"You're not safe on your own."

Callum finished sticking on the plaster and let go of her hand. "Haven't you got a boyfriend to take care of you?"

"If I can survive the hazards of the day," Gaby told him scathingly, with a look that left no doubt she was referring to him, "the nights aren't likely to hold any terrors."

His big hand under her chin forced her face up to his. "Don't tempt me, Gaby," he said threateningly, "to show you how much of a hazard I can really be."

Gaby pushed his hand away contemptuously. "Don't play the squire with me, Callum Durrand. You're a fake, and I'm used to the real thing."

But when Gaby saw the flame flicker in his eyes, she wished she'd held her tongue.

ANNE BEAUMONT started out as a Jill-of-all-writing-trades, but she says it was her experience as a magazine fiction editor, buying stories and condensing them for serialization, that taught her to separate the bones of a story from the flesh. In her own writing she starts with her characters—"a heroine I can identify with, then a hero who seems right for her." She says that many writers work in reverse—plot first, then characters. "That's fine," she says. "If we all had the same method, we might all be writing the same books, and what a crashing bore that would be!" In addition to Anne Beaumont's contemporary romance novels, the author has written historicals under the pen name of Rosina Pyatt. She lives on the Isle of Wight, with its sparkling white beaches, and has three children of whom she is immensely proud.

Books by Anne Beaumont

HARLEQUIN PRESENTS
1231—THAT SPECIAL TOUCH

HARLEQUIN ROMANCE
3049—ANOTHER TIME, ANOTHER LOVE

ANNE BEAUMONT

secret whispers

Old Man With Gun

The Mule

Bohemian Rhapsody

Harlequin Books

TORONTO • NEW YORK • LONDON
AMSTERDAM • PARIS • SYDNEY • HAMBURG
STOCKHOLM • ATHENS • TOKYO • MILAN

Harlequin Presents first edition September 1991
ISBN 0-373-11391-9

Original hardcover edition published in 1990
by Mills & Boon Limited

SECRET WHISPERS

CHAPTER ONE

HARRY PRESTON was without doubt the most handsome and distinguished man in the restaurant, and, as the restaurant was on the Left Bank in Paris, that was really saying something. Gaby Warren was aware how many sleek feminine heads surreptitiously turned his way, and she couldn't help but be flattered that his eyes weren't straying from her face.

'You look enchanting, Gaby,' he told her softly as they began the first course. 'So chic. Paris has been good for you.' His hand came across the white damask tablecloth, touched hers briefly, and was withdrawn.

The lurking dimple in her left cheek appeared as she smiled at him. Harry was so nice, she thought, quite the nicest man she'd ever known. He never took advantage of being her boss, as a lot of men would have done. It was one of the things she liked so much about him.

As she returned her attention to her avocado, she thought too that she liked the way he called her enchanting and not beautiful—because that would have been a lie. She did have a vitality that made her appear more attractive than prettier girls, but that was an illusion. When she was viewed dispassionately, only her huge expressive eyes and her mop of glossy brown hair saved her from being plain.

The best that could be said of the rest of her features was that they had a certain impish charm. So, also, did her small and slender figure. Expensively dressed though she was, in a couture suit of brilliant yellow silk, and with her hair drawn back into a chignon because Harry liked it that way, she still had the air of a little girl playing at being grown-up.

She wasn't a little girl, though, and dining intimately by candle-light with Harry was definitely in the grown-up league, full of hidden and exciting undertones. Childishly she wanted to pinch herself to be sure all this was really happening, but she resisted the impulse, not too sure whether the veneer of sophistication she'd acquired in Paris this past year was what Harry was really complimenting.

She mustn't blow her image now. Besides, she had a favour to ask him, and she wasn't at all sure what his reaction would be. It was still early days for them as a twosome, although she'd have to be as thick as two short planks not to know she was being courted.

The business reasons Harry found for his increasingly frequent flying visits were far from valid. He'd never have let her manage the Paris bureau in the first place if she'd needed constant guidance, but she was happy to go along with the charade. It was a useful cover while their relationship slipped pleasantly over the border between the professional and the personal, an unhurried transition admirably suited to two people who had reason to be cautious.

Harry had a broken marriage to get over, and Gaby—well, she had to get over a dream.

Still, Harry was a man and she was a woman, and sooner or later the crunch would come. Meanwhile, it was so beguiling to be courted with old-world finesse. Everything that was feminine within her softened at being cosseted with good wine and good food, at being flattered and approved of.

When she considered how many of her promising relationships had ended in an ignominious struggle to stay out of bed, she wasn't surprised to find herself more than halfway to adoring him. And it was so comforting to know he was more than halfway to adoring her. No—Gaby checked her thoughts. She didn't mean comforting, she meant thrilling. Harry, after all, was such a catch!

Gaby could feel his eyes still on her, so she looked up enquiringly from her avocado, noticing as she did so how the flickering candle-light shone on the silver at his temples. In any other light those silvery strands were barely perceptible in his fair hair, but she found them so attractive, so intriguing.

They reminded her of what a constant wonder it was that a man who could have his pick of beautiful women should have zeroed in on her. But Harry had, and she was happy, so what more could she possibly want?

Not a thing, Gaby decided, and was immediately aware of the depressingly familiar feeling of discontent that bedevilled her whenever she found herself becoming attached to a man. This time, though, she wasn't going to give in to it. She was going to fight—because if ever a man was worth fighting for, it was Harry.

'In fact,' he continued, as though he'd been leisurely making up his mind about something, 'you look the complete *Parisienne*.'

'I'm not called Gabrielle for nothing. I did have a French mother,' she reminded him. Suddenly becoming aware that this was a heaven-sent opportunity to lead up to the favour she had to ask, she added, 'Don't be fooled, though, by the way I look. Most people usually are.'

Surprise registered in Harry's blue eyes. 'What's that supposed to mean?'

'I'm an English rustic at heart.'

'And I'm Gary Glitter,' he responded, his laughter

showing her all too clearly she hadn't made quite the effect she was hoping for.

'No, I'm serious.'

'You must be ahead of me with the wine,' Harry scoffed. 'There's nothing rustic about you. You're my best linguist, my best head-hunter, and wherever I send you you increase business because everybody finds you as enchanting as I do. In fact, I hold you up to the rest of my staff as the prototype of the new European, an example for them all to copy.'

'Grief,' Gaby murmured, momentarily side-tracked, 'how they must hate me.'

'Nonsense. Every company has a star executive, and you're mine. You've worked for me in Brussels, Bonn and Madrid, you've more than justified my faith in letting you manage the Paris bureau this past year, and you're still only twenty-two. That hardly paints a picture of a straw-chewing yokel.'

Gaby's cheeks were glowing at his praise, but she was aware of how far they were straying from the point. Much as she didn't want to spoil the romantic mood, she had to get back to it, and she hid her anxiety behind a fleeting smile as she hazarded, 'Perhaps you don't really know me, just—just my business image.'

'Nonsense,' Harry said again. 'I know you better than anybody.'

His calm certainty was in a measure justified. She'd worked for the Harry Preston Euro Executive Consultancy since she'd left school at eighteen. It was an extremely exclusive staffing agency, dealing only at the top end of the business, and Harry had watched her mature professionally before he'd taken such a personal interest in her.

When he called her his best head-hunter, it was because a lucrative side of the business was finding

suitable executives to fill specific vacancies and per-
suading them to change jobs. It was something Gaby
was very good at, which made her so valuable to Harry.

Also, he'd researched her background thoroughly
before hiring her in the first place. He knew she was so
good at languages because she'd roamed the world with
her ecologist parents. She'd only lived a settled way of
life when she was coming up to fourteen and her
parents reluctantly sent her to boarding school in
England for a more formal education.

A few months later her parents had been killed in a
landslip in South America. There'd been just enough
money to complete her education. She'd spent her
holidays with her grandfather, who'd died just before
she'd started work. Harry had been sympathetic, but
mostly he knew her as an efficient and successful
executive whose one flaw was her susceptibility to
periodic bouts of restlessness.

He blamed these on her 'vagabond' early life, and
teasingly accused her of not being half French at all,
but half gypsy—never suspecting that behind her practical exterior lived a fey and foolish creature who had
never quite grown up.

Gaby didn't want to shock his complacency too
much, so she said with uncharacteristic cautiousness,
'Everybody has unknown areas, Harry. I'm no
exception.'

Harry was eating mussels cooked in butter sauce,
but he paused in extricating a mussel from its shell to
look searchingly at her. 'What are you trying to tell
me, Gaby? I'd appreciate directness.'

No, you wouldn't, she thought, you'd think me a
retarded adolescent, and you'd be right! The story
she'd rehearsed to conceal the truth didn't come as

glibly to her lips as she'd hoped, and she found herself blurting out, 'I'm homesick.'

'*You*?'

It was amazing how much incredulity Harry managed to get into that one word, and she really couldn't blame him. Trying to sound more convincing, she went on in a rush, 'I need a good long break—six weeks if you can manage it. I need to sink up to my ankles in soggy fields, get stung by nettles, chased by wasps, go down with summer flu—you know, suffer through a good old English summer to remind myself how lucky I am to be working in Paris.'

Harry looked stunned, as well he might. He pushed away his plate, sat back in his chair and surveyed her in silence. Gaby's heart sank. It looked as though she'd have to lace her cover story with a little more of the truth, and she'd hoped she wouldn't have to do that.

Finally he said, 'What's got into you tonight? I've shuffled you about Europe to cure your restlessness, but whenever I've suggested bringing you back to England you've resisted the idea. You've always told me you love living abroad, and out of a suitcase. I don't understand the sudden switch. Besides, how can you possibly be homesick? You don't have a home.'

'I do, Harry,' Gaby contradicted quietly, nerving herself to tread dangerously close to forbidden ground. 'It's at Shorelands.'

Suddenly she pushed her own plate away, telling herself she'd lost interest in the avocado now she'd eaten all the crab filling, but it wasn't really that. She was reacting, as she always did, to the odd tingle that touched her spine and shivered through her emotions whenever she thought of Shorelands.

Shorelands and Justin Durand. . .another life, another dream. Unwanted, hopelessly fanciful—and yet still the intensity of feeling she'd experienced there had never been surpassed. It persisted like a secret whisper in her heart that no man had ever managed to silence.

'Shorelands?' Harry questioned. 'I've never heard of the place.'

'It's in Suffolk,' Gaby told him, and then her throat dried as though her heart had broken only yesterday, and she couldn't go on.

She was saved from floundering in her own mixed-up emotions by the waiter swooping to clear away the first course and serve the second. Gaby loved superbly cooked food, and was slender enough to indulge herself, but she was distracted as she selected braised celery, French beans and minted new potatoes from the vegetable dishes held before her.

Both she and Harry were having peppered steaks, but he'd ordered a Moroccan salad to go with his, and while he was being served her thoughts wandered again. She was ruefully aware that the restlessness he believed she suffered from was just her way of dealing with that damnable secret whisper in her heart.

Whenever she became close to a man, the whisper became a clamour, filling her with discontent and driving her away from him. It was clamouring now because she was falling in love with Harry, forcing her to compare what she felt for him with what she'd felt for Justin.

Always before she'd given up and moved on, hoping that if only she could get far enough away from Shorelands, and stay away for long enough, the whisper would die a natural death. It never had. It only called her back to Shorelands, and this time she was going to listen.

She was going back to silence the whisper herself,

because she was almost certain that Harry was the man she wanted to spend the rest of her life with, and she wasn't going to let anything ruin that—especially anything so foolish! She'd been a sentimental idiot for far too long.

Gaby, still bullying herself back into the real world, didn't notice that the waiter had finished serving until Harry jolted her by saying, 'Suffolk? Isn't that where your grandfather lived?' When she nodded, he added, 'I thought so, but I don't recall your breathing a word about Shorelands. Is it a house, a village, or what?'

'It's an ancient manorial estate,' Gaby replied, trying hard to be matter-of-fact about it as she cut into her steak. 'I own a tiny part of it. A gatehouse, actually. Not the principal one by the main gates, but the one at the back, on the seaward side.'

She had a mental picture, blinding in its vividness, of Justin riding through those rusted old gates on his big bay hunter. And of herself lying along the branch of the enormous oak that overhung the driveway, hidden by leaves, and casting spells so that Justin would look up and fall in love with her. He never did, and only the horse had ever sensed she was there.

Gaby was conscious of love and hope and sadness and an inexpressible yearning. She blinked the picture away but the feeling remained, as it always did, and always would until she sold the gatehouse. The gatehouse was the key, she realised now. It gave her a tiny stake in Shorelands, and therefore in Justin, keeping a vital part of her trapped there, giving substance to a romance that existed only in her heart.

'Gaby,' Harry said, the faintest sound of irritation in his voice, 'why have you been so secretive about this gatehouse? I thought the reason you were so restless is because you haven't any roots anywhere. In fact, it's your gypsy streak that bothers me so much. I've never been too sure whether you'd be able to settle permanently when I move the main office from London to Paris next year and live here myself.'

He didn't say 'settle permanently with me' but the implication was there, and Gaby acknowledged it when she replied, 'That's why I have to return to England. I've always been too. . .too sentimental to sell the gatehouse before. Now I think I'm ready, but. . .but I'd like to spend some time there, to be absolutely sure. That's why I need the six weeks.'

'Why should you be sentimental about a gatehouse, and how did you come to own it in the first place?'

Harry was frowning at her, genuinely puzzled, and Gaby knew she had to stop stuttering and make herself sound believable. Still, there was a lot of truth she could tell him, even if it wasn't the whole truth.

'I inherited it from my grandfather,' she replied. 'He was born on the estate, the son of the head gardener, and he became head gardener himself in time. There'd been a Warren at Shorelands almost as long as there had been a Durand—that's the family who owned the manor—so the house by the seaward gates was always known as The Gardener's Gatehouse——'

'Gaby,' Harry interrupted, 'all this is beginning to sound a bit medieval.'

'Well, it *is*,' she replied, feeling a bit irritated herself, 'although the gatehouse isn't anywhere near as old as the manor. It was built in the first half of the last century in the style known as cottage orné. When I first went to stay with Grandad I thought it looked like something out of *Hansel and Gretel*, a sort of fairy-tale place where magical things could happen.'

Harry's frown vanished and he laughed. 'What a quaint child you must have been.'

Gaby couldn't quite bring herself to laugh with him, so she contradicted, 'Not so much a child, Harry, definitely an adolescent. I was fourteen when I went to Shorelands for the first time.'

And found and lost Justin, she added to herself.

'You must have been a very young fourteen, and that I can readily believe,' Harry commented. 'You don't look anywhere near twenty-two now.'

'The way I look often doesn't have anything to do with the way I feel.' Gaby had meant to say that lightly, but it sounded more of a grumble. Then she realised nervousness had made her drink more wine than she'd supposed. She paused while Harry refilled her glass, then added, 'It can be very annoying, being judged wholly by looks.'

That was what Justin had done, whereas if he'd suspected the way she *felt* he would at least have given her a second glance, or maybe several! She would have been given the chance she'd so desperately yearned for.

Harry broke through her thoughts by saying, 'You're becoming enigmatic again, and I still don't know much about this property of yours.'

'Well, the Durands had been squires at the manor for close on three hundred years, and I always felt my arrival was some kind of catalyst. That summer I arrived the family went broke and sold up. Grandad was offered the gatehouse very cheaply because he'd lived in it all his life, and he bought it.'

Gaby noticed Harry had almost finished his steak and she'd hardly touched hers, so she ate for a while before resuming, 'Grandad was never the same after the Durands left. For him it was the end of a tradition, a way of life, and it was the only life he knew. Coming so soon after the death of his son—my father—it was too much for him. I think his heart broke. He wouldn't work for the new owners, although the Hazletts were nice enough, and so he retired. Four years later he died.'

'Leaving the gatehouse to you,' Harry said for her.

'Yes, but I couldn't live in it myself. I'd just left school, I didn't want to go to college, and languages were the only thing I was good at.' Gaby paused and her impish smile lit her face. 'There's not a lot of call for French, German and Spanish in Suffolk so, much as I loved the place, I had to move south.'

Harry's eyebrows were a lot darker than his hair and they moved together in a frown as he asked, 'You're not seriously expecting me to believe you like country life? Not you, Gaby! As I was saying earlier, you're so chic, so much a town bird. You're a successful businesswoman now, too. I can't imagine what you'd do in the country, except perhaps wilt.'

Gaby's little nose wrinkled as she considered this, and her slender fingers played idly with the stem of her wine glass. 'With my chaotic unbringing I don't honestly think I'd *wilt* anywhere,' she replied eventually. 'I'm either naturally adaptable or I learned the knack early on just to be able to survive with my parents. But the gatehouse was the closest I'd ever had to a real home, and although I only spent my school holidays there I've always felt a bit sentimental about it.'

That, surely, would sound credible, she thought, putting down her knife and fork. She'd cleared her plate without being conscious of eating any of it. She always seemed a little out of the world when she thought of Shorelands. Out of my head more likely, she corrected herself ruefully, and smothered a sigh.

At least, she thought she'd smothered it, but Harry

said, 'I find this very disconcerting, Gaby. You really do sound homesick, but surely you don't visualise a life for yourself in *Suffolk*?'

'Not a life, Harry, just six weeks so I can say goodbye to the old place properly.'

'If you feel like that about it, why have you never been back—or have you?' Harry asked.

'No, I've stayed away deliberately, trying to be practical about it. You're going to think me very silly, but it's as if part of me grew up very fast, and the part of me that knew Shorelands didn't grow up at all. Now I think I've finally got myself together enough to sell the gatehouse and be done with it.'

There, she'd finally got it out without mentioning a word of Justin, and she waited anxiously for Harry's reaction. It was swift and warm. 'I don't think you're the least bit silly, Gaby,' he told her. 'You had a lot of traumas in your life at a very vulnerable age, and it was bound to have some effect on you.' He hesitated, then asked, 'Does your decision have anything to do with me?'

First Gaby was conscious of relief, then she realised he was asking for some kind of commitment. She found she was ready to give it and answered, 'Yes, Harry, it does.'

His hand came over and covered hers again, momentarily tightening before he removed it. 'I'm glad. You can have your six weeks. You're due for three weeks in September anyway. I'll have to look at the holiday rosters, but I'm sure three weeks can be tagged on to that.'

'Thanks,' Gaby said gratefully. 'There are quite a few things to be sorted out, and I don't want to do anything in too much of a rush. Most of the furniture in the gatehouse were gifts from the manor from time to time—outdated pieces that are now very valuable. Some of them I want to keep, so there'll be storage to arrange, that sort of thing. . .'

Her voice trailed away because the waiter was back to clear the table again and serve the third course. Both she and Harry had chosen the same cold dessert, ratafia peaches, and as she began to eat Gaby was thinking that it was already the end of July. One more month and she'd be back at Shorelands, breaking its grip over her, laughing at a romance that had never happened, as she should have laughed years ago.

Yes, that was what she had to do. Nothing could survive that sort of laughter, particularly a romantic dream that should have vanished—like all such dreams!—with her adolescence. It wasn't as if she *enjoyed* being an emotional retard. Foolish she might be, but not that foolish.

Harry's thoughts were running along very different lines, and he said, 'You do realise that if you'd sold the cottage when you inherited it four years ago you could have bought a flat in London before prices went completely crazy. It's never good economics to rent a flat, as you did, when you could have owned your own.'

'I know, but I don't have a crystal ball. I didn't know town prices were going to go haywire, and besides, it wouldn't have made any difference. I just couldn't sell the gatehouse then. It was too—too soon.'

'Well, it's no use crying over spilt milk, and the gatehouse must be providing you with a useful extra income.' Harry waited, but when she didn't say anything he pressed, 'You have been renting it out?'

Gaby replied guiltily, 'Up until last summer, yes. Then my tenants moved out. I told Sam Gibson, the local estate agent who is managing things for me, not to let it again because I'd be home to clear out the cottage for sale. Only when it came to it I still wasn't ready, so I went to Rome instead.'

Harry stared at her in silence and, feeling more guilty than ever, Gaby added defensively, 'Well, I *am* studying Italian, so it wasn't an entirely irresponsible thing to do.'

'Good God!' he exclaimed. 'I can't believe a smart businesswoman like you would do such a thing. Only think of the income you've lost! And to let a valuable property go to rack and ruin——'

'It hasn't, Gaby broke in. 'Sam arranged for a woman from the village to clean and air the gatehouse once a month, and he's made regular inspections for any necessary repairs or maintenance. So far there's only been a bit of storm damage, a few tiles off the roof and a branch needing to be lopped off one of the oaks.'

I hope it wasn't the branch I used to lie along to watch for Justin, she thought involuntarily, then promptly changed her mind. Yes, I do hope it was that branch. I hope everything's different when I get back. Surely even a memory can't survive without substance. . .?

'You mean the gatehouse has been *costing* you money?' The incredulous note was back in Harry's voice, pushing Gaby once more back on the defensive.

'Only for the char. Sam's a friend and doesn't charge anything, and the insurance covered the storm damage. All right, so I have to pay for the insurance, but that's neglible. It isn't as if keeping the gatehouse untenanted has pushed me into bankruptcy, so it's no big deal.'

Gaby, aware by the look on Harry's face that she wasn't winning him round, gazed up at him beguilingly from beneath long, dark eyelashes. It was the first time she'd deliberately flirted with him, but this particular look had never let her down before and she was desperate. 'I know I've been foolish, Harry,' she went on softly, 'but I am going to put it right. There's not a lot else I can say. . .'

Harry did soften, but not as much as she'd hoped, although he sounded more mollified when he replied, 'Well, so long as you realise how foolish you've been, there's not a lot else I can say either. Have you got any others secrets I should know about?'

Gaby couldn't honestly say no, and she didn't want to lie to him, so she joked, 'Well, apart from raiding charity boxes and turning into a vampire after dark, I don't think there's much else for you to worry about.'

'Gaby, this isn't a laughing matter.'

'No, but it isn't exactly the end of the world, either, is it?' she suggested gently.

Harry appeared to struggle with himself, then he replied, 'No, of course it's not. You're very young, so it's natural you'll make the occasional mistake. I've always been aware I have to make allowances for that. Sometimes, though, your sense of humour gives an entirely wrong impression of you. If I didn't know you better, I'd think you were irresponsible.'

That was the judgement Gaby had been dreading, but Harry quickly put it right by continuing, 'However, I *do* know you better, so there's no problem there, and I must admit it's your sense of humour that makes you so popular with our clients. Now, about that Halpern vacancy. Have you got anybody lined up yet?'

The change of subject was so deliberate that Gaby knew Harry was uneasy with the facet of herself she'd just revealed. She suspected this was his way of getting across the message that, although sentiment and indecision were permissible in the growing Gaby, they were unacceptable now.

She'd already come to that conclusion by herself, and yet she felt a flutter of panic at the prospect of being practical and decisive all day and every day. She hoped Harry didn't expect that of her, because she wasn't at all sure she could manage it. The fey and dreamy side of her personality could surface any time and anywhere, perhaps even when she was with him. She could be reckless, too, and altogether different from the Gaby Warren he was falling in love with.

Or would that side of her die with the secret whisper in her heart when she sold the gatehouse? Did she want it to? Oh, gosh, she was dithering again, and she mustn't—she mustn't!—because that meant she was listening to the whisper again when she so much needed to smother it.

Gaby felt her panic mounting, and then her eyes fell on the long-stemmed red rose Harry had given her, lying beside her wine glass on the white damask, and her tilting world steadied. She looked up at Harry's distinguished face, listened to his cultured voice, and everything came back into perspective.

This was real romance, adult and dependable, not some figment of her over-fevered imagination. As an adolescent she might have needed Justin, but as a woman she needed Harry. True, they were discussing business problems now, but business had been the cornerstone of their relationship, and the transition into the romantic was all the more satisfactory because it wasn't being forced along at an unnatural pace.

She was so lucky, Gaby told herself, being given this chance to fall slowly and pleasantly in love instead of being precipitated into that state and missing all the thrilling build-up. . .

By the time Harry was drinking his brandy and she her coffee she'd overcome all the tremors to her nervous system which thinking of Shorelands always aroused. When Harry finally looked at his watch, raised rueful eyebrows and paid the bill, she rose from her chair with the slow grace she'd trained herself into instead of the sudden impulsive movements that had once characterised her so much.

Gaby felt positively queenly as she strolled out of the restaurant with Harry's hand under her arm. Little Miss Nobody from Nowhere had finally arrived some- where, and she liked it—she liked it very much. Then she smiled at her own inflated ego, but when they were outside her mood changed.

It was such a perfect July evening, so warm and close that there was almost a tropical velvet quality about it. Always susceptible to atmosphere, she said impul- sively, 'Oh, Harry, let's walk along the Seine for a little way. Just for a few minutes. You'll still have time to catch your flight.'

'Only if I fall aboard, and I prefer not to be rushed,' Harry replied. 'Do you mind dreadfully?'

'No—no, of course not,' Gaby told him, quickly enough to be reassuring and to smother her disappoint- ment at the same time. It would have been so romantic to stroll beside the lovely river with Harry, a delightful memory to store against those other memories she was bound to stir up when she returned to Shorelands.

But not for the life of her did she know what she had to feel despondent about. There was nothing more romantic than a busy and handsome man flying specially to Paris just to take her to dinner! She waited while Harry asked the doorman in French as perfect as her own to call two taxis, then she said, 'You're not still cross with me for being sentimental about the cottage and wanting an extended leave to put it right?'

'I was never cross, just surprised,' Harry murmured,

kissing her cheek as the first of the taxis pulled up. 'The sooner the matter's settled, the better, so you can pencil in from the beginning of September to mid October.'

'You'll be able to come up to visit me,' Gaby replied softly, anxious to point out at least one advantage of her long leave. 'It will be a lot less hassle than plane-hopping.'

'I'll try, but I'll be spending a lot of time in Rome setting up the new bureau, remember.'

Gaby did remember, and with a certain amount of regret. She'd been studying hard to add Italian to her list of languages, hoping for a posting there, but now that Harry envisaged both their futures in Paris the possibility was remote. Still, she would be gaining far more than she lost.

And they could always honeymoon in Italy, she thought, when Harry handed her into the taxi as his own pulled up behind. Italy was a lot further from Shorelands than France, after all—and then she was appalled to find what lines her mind was running on.

With Harry, it didn't matter how far or how close she was to Shorelands. It was just that secret whisper in her heart spreading doubts where none existed. Well, almost none, and as soon as she was free of Shorelands she would be wholly Harry's.

That was a better thought to take home with her than the memory of a romantic stroll along the Seine. 'Safe flight,' she murmured, 'and thank you for a lovely evening, Harry.'

'My pleasure. I'll see you again just as soon as I can manage it.'

The door closed and the taxi moved off. Gaby turned to wave, but Harry was already getting into the other taxi. Her slender fingers caressed the soft petals of the rose he had given her, and she smiled. This was romance—a snatched meeting, a red rose and the feeling that everything had ended too soon.

Shorelands and Justin were nothing compared to it. But then, at the two magical words, her heart began beating to its own wayward rhythm again, and sending out its own treacherous messages. . .and Gaby, not for the first time, knew what it was to despair.

CHAPTER TWO

ANOTHER nice thing about Harry was that he believed in spending lavishly to create the right setting for his highly successful business. He also believed in using the same equipment and the same décor for his offices in the various European capitals, so that staff and clients moving from one to the other felt instantly in familiar surroundings.

So Gaby, sitting next day at her large designer desk in her blue and yellow designer office, had the comfort of knowing Harry would be working in a similar setting in London. She tried to make her mind dwell on that. It made her feel closer to him, and she desperately needed to feel close to him just then.

After allowing her memories of Shorelands and Justin Durand to surface, she was predictably plagued with restlessness. The month before her leave was due to start seemed to stretch endlessly before her, and in this particular mood work became a bore and not a boon. She was too fidgety, too impatient.

In the quieter moments of her busy schedule she began preparing a brief for her replacement. It was too soon, and would be hopelessly out of date by the time September came, but it was a valiant attempt to settle herself down and keep her mind from wandering where it had no place to be.

By mid-afternoon she was thinking gloomily that she might just as well have spared herself the effort and taken the day off, because her concentration was shot to pieces. In desperation she tried to hold on to an image of Harry's fair and distinguished good looks, but the image wouldn't hold true. It kept blurring and changing into a younger and altogether different face.

No matter how many times she blinked her eyes or shook her head, she still saw the straight black eyebrows, the dark-lashed brown eyes, the firm chin and nose, the overlong thick black hair, and most of all the devastating swift white smile of Justin Durand.

At fourteen, Gaby mused, her pen making doodles instead of pertinent remarks on her report, I never stood a chance. It was inevitable that once I saw him I would tumble helplessly in love with him. He might have been an unreachable twenty-two, and already knee-deep in swooning girls closer to his age, but he was the mythical hero every schoolgirl dreams of come to life, and I did more dreaming than most. . .

Gaby, giving up any attempt to write and nibbling the end of her pen, thought that all Justin had lacked that summer when she was fourteen was a suit of shining armour, and she'd been so bedazzled she'd never missed it anyway. What a moonstruck moron she must have seemed to him! No wonder he'd never realised he was supposed to come charging up on his big bay hunter and carry her off to the medieval manor where they would live happily ever after.

To him she'd just been the gardener's quaint and tongue-tied granddaughter, half child and half woman, no heroine worthy of being rescued from her misery. So she'd spun her own romances around him, and that was all right—except that they'd become more real to her than reality, which wasn't all right at all.

Gaby, sighing, tried to smile at her own absurdity, but she only felt resentful. Why did she have to be so different? Why couldn't she have fallen at that hopelessly romantic age for a pop or film star, as other girls

did? Somebody whose picture she could have cut from
a magazine, who would have married or aged or fallen
from grace in some other way, so that disenchantment
would have come naturally and not too painfully.

Oh, no, nothing so reasonable for her! She had to
land herself with a dream that was frozen in time—and
became a nightmare when she fell for somebody else.
She must be really weird, or a masochist.

But Gaby, chewing harder on her pen, didn't feel
either. She just felt very vulnerable as she began to
ache again with the bittersweet sadness of her first, and
Justin's last, summer at Shorelands. She remembered
the hope of the succeeding summers when she'd
returned to Grandad's gatehouse, praying that by some
miracle Justin would be there.

Every summer she'd been one year older, cutting the
gap in maturity between her fourteen and his twenty-
two, so she'd been absolutely certain they'd meet again
at some point in time that was absolutely right for
them.

But they never had. The Durands, when they sold
Shorelands, had left for good. Justin had disappeared
into New York. His parents had retired to a Greek
island. Gaby had got their address from Mrs Hoskins,
the housekeeper who'd remained to work for the
Hazletts, and had written to tell them of her grandfather's death.

They'd sent a suitable letter of condolence, and a
mail-order wreath, but they hadn't felt obliged to
attend the funeral themselves. Gaby had been disappointed for Grandad's sake, because she knew he'd
have expected them to be there. Justin she hadn't tried
to contact, thinking him the wrong generation to be
concerned with *noblesse oblige*.

Justin must, Gaby thought sorrowfully, have been

glad to escape the weight of a medieval inheritance to have gone so far and to have stayed away so obdurately. How strange it was that she, who'd never really belonged at Shorelands, was the only one who'd never managed to break free.

Wherever he was now, Justin would be thirty. The insuperable age gap had become just the right sort of difference, except that she was returning to Shorelands to free herself for marriage with somebody else. Which was as it should be. Dreams might not change, but people did.

Gaby, uncertain whether she'd changed as much as she should have done, found herself staring out of her window at a leafy chestnut tree that shaded her office from the fierce afternoon sun. Impulsively she went over and opened the window, knowing it would play havoc with the air-conditioning, but suddenly she felt unbearably closed in.

She needed to see the sky, but what with the buildings and the tree she had to lean out and crane her head sideways to catch a glimpse of blue. It wasn't enough, and she knew she was yearning for the wide skies of Suffolk and air she could breathe, really breathe, with the crisp tang of salt on it straight from the North Sea.

So she hadn't been lying when she'd told Harry she was homesick last night. . . . She really was, only it was all mixed up with memories of Justin and Shorelands and her own indecision over the gatehouse. As Gaby drew back into her office and closed the window on that disappointing patch of pallid blue above, the month before her leave was due took on the burden of a year.

The phone rang as she sat down again at her desk, and she almost snatched it up, grateful at having her moody thoughts interrupted. It was Harry, and her mood veered from despondency to pleasure. 'Sleep well last night, Gaby?' he asked softly.

'Like a top,' she lied, because her night had been as restless as her day. 'Did you have a good flight?'

'Just about perfect.' Harry's tone changed as though, the pleasantries over, he was in a hurry to get to the point. 'Gaby, I've shuffled the holiday roster about, and it will be easier if you take your leave earlier rather than tag the extra weeks on the end. How do you feel about that?'

Gaby felt a surge of excitement and she found it difficult to match Harry's businesslike manner as she replied, 'That will suit me fine.'

'Good. Sonia, who's a trainee manager here in London, and Cheryl at the Madrid bureau, are both skiing fanatics, so they're booked for winter holidays. I propose sending Sonia to Madrid to get her first taste of relief work, and Cheryl to Paris to replace you. Madrid's quiet at this time of year, and Paris isn't exactly hopping, either, so I reckon they'll both be able to cope. It will be good experience for both of them, and will release you almost immediately.'

'How immediately?' Gaby asked, wondering if Harry was more tuned in to her thoughts and feelings than she'd suspected.

'Sonia can fly to Madrid tonight, and Cheryl can be in Paris by Thursday morning for her briefing, so you can take off Friday. Can you organise yourself by then?'

'I certainly can,' Gaby responded, her excitement spilling over into her voice. Today was Monday, leaving just three more days before she would be on her way to Shorelands. Even her acute restlessness couldn't quibble at that. She would have all of August and the first two weeks in September to get all that sort of nonsense out of her system. She added gratefully, 'Thanks for moving so fast, Harry. I didn't expect——'

'No thanks necessary,' he broke in, then his voice altered again as he went on, 'I don't like the feeling that I'm sharing you with something else, even if it's only a gatehouse. As I said last night, the sooner the business is settled, the better, and not only from a financial point of view.'

'You're right,' Gaby told him softly. 'I've dithered too long.'

'That's my girl. Unfortunately, I'm flying to Rome on Thursday so I won't see you when you come through London. Do you want me to arrange overnight accommodation for you in a hotel, or would you like the use of Sonia's bedsit?'

It was normal practice when the girls replaced each other in their jobs that they also used each other's accommodation, but Gaby had no need of it this time. 'If you won't be in London, Harry, I might as well push straight on for Shorelands.'

There it went again, that odd tingle along her spine that set all her nerve-ends quivering when she mentioned Shorelands, and guiltily she rushed on, 'I'm sorry I'll be missing you. How long will you be in Rome?'

'A fortnight, possibly three weeks. Is the gatehouse on the phone?'

'No, but there's a pub nearby—the Fisherman's Dream, at Shevingham. I'll arrange it so you can leave a message for me there if you need to, otherwise I'll be in touch when I have something constructive to report,' Gaby said.

'Right. I'll be up to see you as soon as I can manage

it, in any case.' Another phone in Harry's office began
to ring and he ended hastily, 'Take care, Gaby.'

'I will,' she promised, and the line went dead.

When she replaced the receiver she found herself
smiling foolishly at it, as thrilled as she'd ever been as
a schoolgirl at the prospect of returning to Shorelands
for the summer. For years she'd forced herself to stay
away in an attempt to break its spell, and here she was
right back at square one. But no, she thought, that
really wasn't what her smile was all about.

It was about Harry saying, 'I don't like the feeling
that I'm sharing you. . .'

Gaby picked up Cheryl from the airport just before ten
on Thursday morning and drove back to her little flat
to offload the suitcases before taking her on to the
office. 'This is cute,' Cheryl said, opening the french
windows in the sitting-room and leaning over the
flower-filled balcony to look down at the busy street
four storeys below.

'I like it,' Gaby replied, a bit breathless after carrying
one of the suitcases up the narrow flights of stairs. 'I'd
like it better if it had a lift, but at least there's plenty
of space once I get up here. I don't like feeling
cramped. It's not exactly convenient for the office, but
there's the Metro a couple of streets away. I'll show
you when I drive you in.'

'Ah.' Cheryl came back into the flat and closed the
windows behind her. 'Does that mean I don't get the
use of your car as well as the flat?'

'I'm afraid not. I'm taking it back to England with
me. I'll need it in Suffolk. It's pretty rural where I'm
going. Well, if you're fit, I'll take you into the office
for your briefing. Just about everybody who's anybody
migrates from Paris in August, so you should have a

relatively quiet time. Things will buck up in September, of course, but I'll be back on the fourteenth.'

'Don't hurry on my account,' Cheryl said, smiling. 'I don't care if you never come back. I'd be only too happy to filch your job permanently. I love Paris—and French is my best language.'

'How's your German coming along?' Gaby asked as she led the way out of the flat and down the stairs. The girls had met when Cheryl joined the consultancy three years ago, and their paths had crossed several times since.

Cheryl pulled a face. 'I'm happier with the Latin languages. How's your Italian?'

'Dependable,' Gaby replied, unlocking the door of her silver Volkswagen Golf. Then she added incautiously, 'If I ever get to use it.'

Cheryl was on to that in a flash. 'What do you mean? I thought you were earmarked for the new Rome bureau Harry's setting up.'

'Well, nothing's ever too certain, is it?' she replied hastily. 'I expect my restless feet will take me there one day, but I love Paris too, you know.'

To look at, Cheryl was as different from Gaby as it was possible to be, a tall and statuesque blue-eyed blonde, but she certainly wasn't stupid, nor could she be easily side-tracked. As she strapped herself into her seat while Gaby eased the car into the traffic, she shot a sidelong look at her and asked bluntly, 'Gaby, is something going on between you and Harry? I've heard a few rumours. . .'

'Office gossip,' Gaby replied dismissively. 'I'd have thought you'd been with the firm long enough to not take any notice of those.'

'Well, now the consultancy is expanding so rapidly he says it will be more convenient to control things from Paris, and here's you sounding doubtful about going to Rome when everybody knows you're set on that posting.'

'*Was* set,' Gaby corrected. 'I'm not as restless as I used to be.'

'You mean you're ready to settle down?' Cheryl asked. Then, more pertinently, 'With Harry?'

Gaby laughed, she hoped convincingly, because both she and Harry had been so careful not to set tongues wagging before they were sure of each other. It could be so difficult if things didn't work out. A mutual rejection would be all right, but, since he was her boss, if one rejected the other an embarrassing situation could arise. It was one of the reasons why they were being so cautious.

'Harry's still smarting from his divorce,' she replied, 'and we're just a good working team. Come on, Cheryl, you know better than to read anything more into it than that.'

'His divorce was two years ago and he's been making a lot of trips to Paris,' Cheryl mused with another of her sidelong looks.

'So? Before things eased with the summer breaks there were a lot of tricky negotiations going on here.'

'Which you're perfectly competent to deal with. Harry's always singing your praises,' Cheryl persisted.

'Don't hate me for that. I'm not too proud to shout for help if I need it. Harry knows that, which is why he trusts me so much.'

'Hah!' Cheryl snorted sceptically. 'Suddenly you ask for a six-week holiday and you get it, just like that, even if it means hurling the rest of the staff about Europe like ping-pong balls.'

'You're exaggerating,' Gaby scoffed. 'Didn't Harry tell you why I need a long leave?'

'He's the boss. He doesn't have to explain anything to me, does he? He just told me to clue up Sonia when she arrived in Madrid, and then get my butt on a plane to Paris.'

'I'm sure he didn't put it as crudely as that,' Gaby replied, with a genuine laugh this time. 'Harry wouldn't know how to be less than a gentleman. The fact is, my grandfather died and left me a quaint old gatehouse in Suffolk. I'm going back to sell it. There's furniture to be sorted out and sold or stored, as well, and the extra time means I won't have to do it all in one mad rush.'

No need to tell Cheryl she'd owned the gatehouse for four years, or that her involvement with Harry had forced her to stop dithering about it, Gaby thought. As with Harry, she wasn't lying precisely, she just wasn't telling the whole truth.

'So *that's* what it's all about!' Cheryl exclaimed. 'We were all scenting a big romance. Well, I'm sorry your job's not up for grabs, but I'm glad Harry still is. Now there's a man to fantasise about!'

Gaby, safe in the knowledge she would be doing more than fantasising about Harry once she put a stop to her silly fantasies about Justin, steered the conversation towards business, and since Cheryl wanted to do well in Paris she had no trouble keeping it there.

It wasn't until the evening, when Gaby took Cheryl to a little restaurant close to the flat where the food was excellent and didn't cost the earth, that the talk became personal again. Cheryl started it by asking, 'How do you see yourself in the long term—as the career or the marrying type?'

We're getting back to Harry, Gaby thought, squeezing lemon juice on to her sole meunière. Cheryl's got a bee in her bonnet about him, and it's going to keep buzzing away until she gets the answers she wants.

Well, she isn't going to get them. 'Isn't it a bit quaint to think of it in either-or terms?' Gaby hedged. 'Women manage both successfully these days.'

'Yes, but I think we're still basically one type or the other,' Cheryl persisted, her blue eyes beaming in on Gaby's face in a way that made her feel she was under a microscope.

'Maybe you are, but I don't think of myself in terms of type,' Gaby retorted, wrinkling her little nose as though she found the idea distasteful. 'It's too restricting. I'm more a creature of whim. I do what I want when I want to, without bothering about what effect it will have on the next fifty years.'

'Harry wouldn't think that a very positive attitude, and he's very hot on positive attitudes.'

'You worry about that, and I'll go my own sweet way as usual,' Gaby told her lightly.

'It's because you get your own sweet way so often that the rest of us think Harry's hot on you as well,' Cheryl said, abandoning guile for bluntness. 'Sonia was telling me how many trips he's made to Paris lately, and she doesn't think all of them could have been business.'

'Sonia should take it up with Harry,' Gaby retorted drily, 'although I wouldn't presume to pry into his private life, and I've worked for him longer than either of you.'

'You mean he's seeing somebody else here?'

Gaby shrugged. 'I'm certainly not sleeping with him. Are you?'

'Of course I'm not!'

'Well, then, what's all the big fuss about?' Gaby asked.

'There's no fuss—just curiosity.'

'Which killed the cat,' Gaby promptly replied, and they both laughed.

All in all, Gaby thought, settling down to sleep on the sofa in the living-room later that evening because she'd given over her bed to Cheryl, I brushed through that pretty well. But it was obvious that she and Harry hadn't been as clever as they'd supposed, and if they delayed making up their minds much longer the secret would be an open one.

It was her last thought that night. She fell asleep promptly, which was a good thing, the alarm being set to wake her before dawn. Half an hour later, with her passport in her handbag and her suitcases in the back of the car, she was driving through the empty streets of Paris. She had the windows open, but the heat of yesterday seemed trapped between the buildings, making it oppressive and heavy, and she found herself yearning once more to breathe in the clear, bracing air of Shorelands.

She drove fast and expertly, full of anticipation, and with the strangest feeling that she hadn't a minute to lose—which, she told herself, was quite crazy. Having stayed away from Shorelands for four years, an hour more or less wasn't going to make any difference.

She was one of the first aboard the ferry at Calais, and when she drove off at Dover, clearing Customs without any problems, she began the two-hundred-mile journey that would take her home with the same fresh eagerness with which she'd left Paris.

Except, of course, that Shorelands had never been her home, and now never would be. Home is where the heart is, her brain mocked, but she shrugged the old saying away. Harry had half of her heart. When she retrieved the other half he would have that, too.

She would be a whole person again, capable of loving completely, capable of expressing that love freely.

Out of mothballs finally, she thought flippantly, at the grand old age of twenty-two. No wonder she was suddenly in such a tearing hurry. She had missed so much of real living because of her fixation on an adolescent dream, and she didn't want to miss any more. Justin, though he hadn't known it, had been bad for her. Harry, as she was just beginning to fully appreciate, had been nothing but good.

She stopped for an early lunch because she hadn't felt like breakfasting on the ferry, and in the afternoon she stopped again for high tea. Wafer-thin cucumber sandwiches, warm scones dripping with butter and jam and cream, cool strawberries.

Gaby, sated from eating too much and too richly, felt like a schoolgirl again as she continued her journey. Something else was happening to her, as well. Like the chameleon she was, always sensitive to her surroundings, she was shedding her French image. She was becoming again the English rustic Harry refused to believe existed, her soft brown eyes drinking in the rich green fields grazed by docile cattle, the acres of ripening wheat and corn and barley, the graceful willows shading slow-running rivers.

The secret whisper in her heart was happy now, and it was only as the landmarks became familiar and she closed on Shorelands in the late afternoon that nebulous but nagging fears beset her. Four years was a long time to stay away. What if everything had changed?

With so much property development going on, Shorelands could be one vast estate of little square houses with little square gardens for all she knew. No more meadows heavy with dew, full of wild flowers and the flutter of delicate butterfly wings, no more little coppices and grander woods, perhaps even no more marshes thick with wildfowl and busy with the flash of kingfishers, swallow-tails and dragonflies.

Gaby's heart almost stopped at the thought, and when it started again its beat was painful, full of anxiety. She had always thought of Shorelands as timeless, wrapped in its medieval trance, inviolate. But there were no Durands to watch over it any more.

The Hazletts were a pleasant elderly couple, but they weren't farmers. Shorelands was nothing but a retirement haven to them. They'd leased out the land of the home farm, and the other two supporting farms had been sold separately. Gaby realised with increasing dread that she was probably the only one left who cared deeply about it, and she'd spent the last four years trying not to care at all.

What is it with me? she asked herself crossly. Justin or Shorelands? It wasn't a question she could answer. In her mind the two were inextricably mixed, and her heart had to be purged of both. Still, as she came over the brow of a gentle hill and looked down into the wide valley, telling herself it would be so much easier for her if everything had changed, she was conscious of inexpressible relief when she saw that nothing had.

The manor house itself was hidden behind a great stand of oak, ash and birch, but no housing or industrial sprawl marred the fields and meadows. Away to the west the quaint little village of Shevingham, with its mellowed mixture of Tudor and Georgian houses, looked unchanged, and Gaby's fears fell from her.

She'd been like an imaginative child, frightening herself with bogies that didn't exist. Shorelands, still weaving its timeless magic, looked as though it was waiting for her—but then, she'd always fancied that.

I'm half fey and half foolish, she nagged herself. Harry wouldn't approve. In fact, he wouldn't even know me. What am I going to do about this side of me which I can't control? Kill it, of course, a wiser Gaby argued back, that's what you're here for. Somehow, though, it had been easier to be wise in Paris than now, when she was actually here at Shorelands.

A light breeze was sending tufts of cloud sailing like stately galleons across the wide sky she remembered so well, bringing with it the fresh tang of the sea she'd yearned for. She couldn't have chosen a finer day to return. Everything was perfect. Perhaps too perfect?

Reaction set in and Gaby laughed at herself. First she'd been worried in case everything was spoiled, and now she was worrying because nothing had. If she didn't watch herself, she'd end up on a psychiatric couch, and she wouldn't be able to quibble about belonging there!

Gaby was still smiling as she turned off the main road along a high-hedged lane that twisted and turned its way towards the manor and the sea. Another memory came back to tease and provoke her. It was of Justin driving his low and lethal-looking sports car along this lane, herself pressed back against the hedge as he passed without a backward glance. The spoilt young man who'd had everything and then found himself with virtually nothing.

Had he been truly grateful to have a medieval burden lifted from his shoulders, or had it been sorrow that had driven him all the way to America? She'd never been close enough to him to ask, and had been too shy to question anybody else, fearful that she might reveal how much she adored him. She wanted to laugh at herself now, but at the time she couldn't have borne anybody else laughing at her.

As she drove over a hump-backed bridge, on for several hundred yards and then down through a water-splash, Gaby's spine began to tingle in the old familiar way. She knew she was sensing Justin's presence, but she told herself briskly that it was only because she was a sponge when it came to soaking up atmosphere. It was a talent—more likely a curse!—that she really wished she'd been spared. It only highlighted how nobody complicated her life quite like herself.

She slowed as she approached the high wall that enclosed the manor house, its farm and parklands. The great wrought-iron main gates were freshly painted black, and the Durand coat of arms incorporated in them gleamed red, white and gold. Gaby was surprised. She could see that the old wall had been repaired and refaced, too, but, now that the Hazletts had finally got round to obliterating signs of decay, she'd imagined they'd have had the Durand crest painted out. Not so, obviously, although she'd never suspected they were snobs happy to bathe in reflected glory.

Through the gates she glimpsed its guardian house, much bigger than her own and also recently redecorated. She wondered if Mrs Hoskins, the Durands' and then the Hazletts' housekeeper, still lived there with her husband Tom, whom she remembered seeing occasionally in formal butler's black, but more often in the dungarees of a general handyman.

The Hoskinses slid from Gaby's mind as she continued on what was little more than a track now circling the high wall, the smooth tarmac ending at the main gates to the manor. The grassy banks on either side were thick with cow parsley, orange-centred daisies and the blues, yellows and purples of other wild flowers her grandfather had painstakingly taught her the names of.

She knew the fine weather must have lasted for some time, because the track, which she remembered as being sometimes glutinous with mud, was baked hard and the car jolted and dipped over the lumps and bumps. Gaby didn't mind. It was all a part of coming home at last. She felt so deep in the past that she imagined she could hear hoofbeats on the other side of the wall.

More foolishness, of course. It was years since Justin had ridden to the seaward gates and the stables had stood empty since he'd left, the Hazletts having no love of horses.

The tiredness that had been creeping up on Gaby after her long day's travelling vanished in a surge of excitement as she finally approached the driveway to her own gatehouse. She began to swing the wheel to enter, and then slammed on the brakes.

The old gates lolling drunkenly on broken hinges were gone. A new set replaced them and they were closed. What was more, the damaged kestrels—emblem of the Durands—on top of each supporting pillar had been replaced by a brand-new pair. Gaby blinked at them, and could only suppose that the Hazletts were now seriously identifying with the Durands and were bent on restoring all their vanished glory.

She got out of her car, grasped the gates and rattled them. There was no give. They were firmly bolted on the inside. Balked, she stepped back and noticed a door for pedestrians set in the right-hand gate. She tried that, but it was just as firmly locked. A new notice-board fixed to the right-hand pillar caught her attention and she read, 'Shorelands Manor. Enquire at Main Gates.' There was an arrow beneath it pointing back the way she'd come.

Through the bars of the gates she could see her gatehouse. It looked forlorn and unloved, with its shuttered windows downstairs and its latticed windows upstairs dustily reflecting the sun. The white paint was peeling from the fancy wooden fretwork that decorated the cottage like icing on an over-elaborate birthday cake, and the garden was a hopeless tangle of overgrown flowers and weeds. This was her home, though, and it wasn't right that she should be locked out of it.

In fact, it was a liberty, Gaby thought grimly. The Hazletts had overreached themselves. She was guaranteed proper access to the gatehouse in the deeds. She was certain of that, because she'd read them carefully before handing them over to her lawyer for safe keeping.

She was angry, and she grasped the gates again and rattled them in sheer frustration. When she stopped the hoofbeats she'd thought she'd heard while driving around the estate became louder. They were definitely real, and no mere figment of her imagination as she'd supposed because she was once more back within the magic aura of Shorelands.

She stood stock-still, a slight and trembling figure locked outside the gates, her eyes growing huge in her wistful face as a rider approached. She saw a huge blue roan, at least seventeen hands, built for stamina and not for style like the handsome bay she remembered.

But the rider. . .the straight back, the set of the shoulders, the way his head was held and that unruly mop of black hair. . .no, it couldn't possibly be! Not now, when she was going to sell her Hansel and Gretel gatehouse because she'd stopped believing in fairytales. Justin was gone, irrevocably lost to her!

But the secret whisper in her heart knew better, and was already bursting into song.

CHAPTER THREE

GABY'S heart had made no mistake, and now her eyes confirmed that this was indeed Justin, returned by some miracle to Shorelands. The smooth handsome face she remembered was seasoned with lines of experience about the eyes and mouth, but everything else about him was the same.

Gaby felt her legs trembling in earnest, and she was clasping the bars of the gate so fiercely that her knuckles whitened. She tried to get a grip on herself, but her heart wouldn't stop singing and her brain wouldn't stop telling her that she'd always known this would happen—that they'd meet again when the time was right for them.

Harry, and all the other men her instincts had stopped her getting too closely involved with, might never have existed. She was breathless, expectant, not knowing what would happen, only certain that this was the most important moment of her life.

Justin checked his horse before the gate, turned it sideways as he released the bolt and then backed the horse away as Gaby pushed her way through. 'Hello,' he said, with that easy smile she remembered so well, although it had rarely been bestowed on her. 'Are you another lost tripper? If you're looking for Shevingham, I'm afraid you'll have to go back the way you came, turn right and then keep on going until you reach the main road. This is a private road, but there's a signpost at the crossroads before Shevingham which will tell you how to reach the sea, if that's what you want.'

'Justin,' Gaby said, a tremor in her voice she couldn't quite control. 'It's me.'

The black eyebrows shot up and a smile touched his lips. 'I can see it is—but who's me?'

'Gaby.'

'I'm sorry. It's a long while since I've been in these parts, and I can't seem to remember. . .' His eyebrows stayed up quizzically.

'Gaby Warren.' She wasn't surprised he didn't remember her, but she was piqued that the name didn't ring a bell, because he still looked puzzled. She added a little crossly, 'The gardener's granddaughter.'

'Good grief, Gaby Warren! You're the little waif the old boy took in the summer my family sold up and left. You were orphaned and came here for the boarding school hols.'

'That's right,' Gaby replied, none too pleased to hear her grandfather referred to as 'the old boy'.

Justin smiled disarmingly and went on, 'You were such a funny little thing, all wistful eyes and wild hair, and forever popping up in unexpected places. I used to think you were haunting me and wondered if you were a throwback to the woodwose.'

Gaby laughed; she couldn't help herself. The woodwose were the little people who were supposed to have lived in the fens way back in the mists of time. She'd seen carved images of them on the door-knockers of old houses and at the ends of pews in ancient churches. She wrinkled her little nose and protested, 'That's not very flattering.'

'Don't worry, you've improved a hundred per cent.' Justin began to circle the blue roan around her, studying her in a frankly appreciative way. 'Still mostly eyes and hair, I see, but cute as well. You can haunt me as much as you like now. I'll be back to encourage you. You and I are definitely going to get better acquainted.'

The flash of a smile and he stopped circling the roan and went through the gate. Gaby called after him, 'Justin, have you got Shorelands back? I noticed the family crest has been repainted on the main gates, and the kestrels have been renewed here. I thought it funny the Hazletts should——'

She got no further. Justin glanced back, the smile gone, a frown marring his handsome face. 'No, Shorelands isn't mine, I'm just a guest here. You own more of it than I do—not that you're likely to for very much longer.'

He touched his heels to the big roan's flanks, every inch the romantic figure she remembered in his tailored jodhpurs and expensive white shirt. Gaby stared after him in bewilderment, her high spirits plummeting. For a few precious minutes Justin had seemed as unchanged and as carelessly romantic as ever, and she'd dared to hope this was the magic summer she'd always dreamed of, when they'd finally meet here at Shorelands as a man and a woman.

But the magic was flawed. Shorelands wasn't his, as it should be, and beneath the smiling face he had shown her he was bitter and angry. Her heart ached for him and her arms ached to comfort him. She couldn't give him Shorelands, but she could give him consolation if he would let her.

Suddenly resolute, Gaby opened the gates wide and drove the car through, swinging it expertly into the weed-filled driveway and stopping in front of the garage that stood separate from the gatehouse. It was little more than a wooden shack her grandfather had built himself, but her mind wasn't on that.

As she got out of the car she knew that Justin would

come to her, if not for comfort then for something else. She was a grown woman now, and she'd seen that look in his eyes too many times to be mistaken. He found her desirable and she wouldn't disappoint him. She'd waited too long for this time and this place. . .and for Justin.

There was a little smile on her lips as she pulled her handbag from her car and turned away. She couldn't find the path that led from the garage to the front door. It was lost somewhere under clumps of nettles and white daisy-like chrysanthemums, so she walked back along the driveway, round the low brick wall that edged the garden to the main path. This was paved and usable, and the clematis, honeysuckle and roses that grew over the front porch had been kept in some sort of order, but only just. The char she employed clearly didn't believe in doing any more than she absolutely had to outside the house.

Gaby delved into her handbag for the key and tried, then tried again, to put it in the lock, but it wouldn't go. It took her a while to realise the reason, but when she did she was angry. What a cheek! Somebody had changed the lock! Scarcely able to believe it, she fought her way through the tangled briars and bushes to reach the back door, only to find the lock had been changed there as well.

She stood back and stared up at the house as though, if she only stared long enough, it would tell her what had been going on here. Not surprisingly, it didn't, and with an angry exclamation she fought her way once more through the undergrowth to the shuttered kitchen window. She unlatched and open the shutters and a large spider, rudely dislodged, fell towards her feet.

Gaby squealed and jumped sideways, catching her foot in a briar and tumbling on her side. The hand she put out to save herself landed on a wickedly thorned trailing rose. She felt more thorns tear her leg and squealed again, this time with pain. When she stood up her hand and leg were bleeding and she was no closer to getting inside her home.

She wished Justin hadn't ridden away so abruptly. If he were here to help her get into the gatehouse she wouldn't care how long it took, or how much she got scratched, but as it was weariness overtook her. She was hot, she was hungry, and she felt like bursting into tears.

This, she told herself like the well-trained executive she was, is an entirely negative and unproductive reaction! Do something positive! The spider had vanished, but she shivered at the thought of it running around her feet without her being able to see it. Gingerly she stepped up to the window and inspected it more closely. It was shut and latched.

The sensible thing to do would be to drive up to the manor house and ask the Hazletts what the devil they thought they were doing with her property, but she didn't want her homecoming, which had started so auspiciously, to degenerate into an almighty row. Not so soon, anyway.

The kitchen window opened outwards and, rummaging in her handbag for a nail file, Gaby slid it up the vertical join hoping to dislodge the latch. She was so engrossed in what she was doing that she was taken completely by surprise when an arm like iron came around her waist and she was yanked away.

She screamed, found herself lifted off her feet and, dangling helplessly under her attacker's arm, she was carried struggling and kicking through the garden and dumped outside the big iron gates again. They clanged shut behind her. Breathless, her mind not reacting fast enough to what had happened to her, she landed off balance, staggered, and heard a voice she knew so well say icily, 'If those long-haired louts you run around with thought I'd be softer on you, you can tell them how wrong they are. I warned the lot of you what would happen if I caught you on my land again. Now you'll have to pay!'

Gaby turned, dazedly shaking back the long thick hair that had fallen across her face during the rough treatment she'd suffered. Through it, and through the close-set bars of the gates, she saw him and stuttered indignantly, 'J-Justin! Have you gone mad?'

'I'm not Justin.'

Gaby blinked in bewilderment, not for the first time that day. She felt bruised and battered, and she lifted trembling hands to push back the last of the hair from her face. She'd returned to Shorelands, and it seemed she was some sort of catalyst again because the whole world had run crazy.

But her vision was clear now, her brain had begun to work again and she saw that the brute on the other side of the gates wasn't Justin. He was so like him, though, that she wondered whether she'd had a knock on the head and her intense inner yearning was conjuring him up wherever she looked.

No, that wasn't the answer. She wasn't quite that crazy yet. This brute had the same black hair, the same cast of features, but he was bigger, broader, and his eyes were a flinty blue to Justin's melting brown. Gaby didn't know what to say—not that she was given any chance to say anything.

'If you're not one of those damned squatters, what are you?' he asked contemptuously. 'One of Justin's women? If you and he are planning to use the gate-house as a love-nest, he could at least have told you where to find the key.'

Gaby's face flamed. Completely forgetting in her
fury how much she yearned for Justin's arms around
her, she denied hotly, 'I'm not one of his women! I
own the gatehouse! What the blazes do you think
you're doing, denying me access to my property and
behaving as if it's your own? I suppose it was you who
changed the locks!'

'Yes.'

'You've got a nerve!'

He opened the gates and stood looking down at her.
She was flushed, dishevelled, bruised, her hand and leg
were stinging from the thorns, and she glowered at
him. But how she looked or what she said seemed to
have no effect on him because, his leisurely inspection
of her finished, he said, 'So you're Gaby Warren. I've
heard about you, but nobody told me you make a lot
of noise for somebody who hasn't anything sensible to
say. If you'd bothered to look after your property I
wouldn't have had to do it for you. I've got better
things to do than chuck out parasitic squatters and
keep an eye on the place.'

Under different circumstances Gaby would have
been grateful, but she was so livid at his rough treatment of her that she'd have willingly died before
admitting a debt to him. 'What goes on in my house is
no concern of yours,' she told him loftily.

'Anybody who trespasses on my land is very much
my concern. I'm fussy whom I allow inside my gates.
You're the only one with legal access, nobody else.'

His land. This man who looked and sounded like a
Durand—but couldn't be one—claimed he owned
Shorelands. What had been going on here? Even
though her mind was whirling with questions, Gaby
stuck to what was most important to her right then,
and replied triumphantly, 'I'm glad you realise that.

Perhaps it will make you stop to consider who's a trespasser and who isn't before you do your gorilla act in future. You had no right whatsoever to throw me out.'

She looked him up and down just as objectionably as he had her. When she considered her point made, she stalked past him towards the gatehouse. She didn't get far. She was swept off her feet again. This time Gaby found herself lying in his arms, which put her in a better position to struggle, and she struggled wildly.

He stood quite still, looking bored while she wore herself out. When she did and stopped wriggling, he said, 'There's a good girl. I knew you'd get the idea eventually.'

Rage boiled up in Gaby again, but she wasn't going through another useless and undignified struggle, so she retorted coldly, 'Are you sure you should be down on the ground and not swinging from the trees?'

'From what I've heard, you're the tree-walker,' he replied cryptically.

Gaby's face flamed. He could only be referring to the way she used to hide in trees to catch a glimpse of Justin, and nobody knew about that, surely? Then she heard an echo of Justin's voice saying just a few minutes ago, 'You were such a funny little thing. . .forever popping up in unexpected places.'

Oh God! Justin must have known all along how her adoration of him had caused her to spy on him. He must have talked about it to this man, joked about it. But why? What possible reason was there for Justin, who'd almost forgotten her, to discuss her with a man who'd never even met her? It didn't make sense.

Sense or not, she felt a momentary surge of hatred for the pair of them, but she forced herself to reply blandly, 'I used to climb trees a lot when I was a kid, if that's what you mean. Who didn't? I'd much rather know what you intend to do with me.'

'Put you back where I found you. As you said, I'd no right to throw you out, and I always like to put a mistake right.' He began striding with her towards the gatehouse, and she thought him the most objectionable and overbearing man she'd ever had the misfortune to meet.

Her small hands clenched into fists, she saw he was watching her with a half-smile, realised that all she was doing was amusing him, and forced her fists to relax. 'Very wise,' he murmured approvingly.

Gaby could willingly have murdered him, and between gritted teeth she asked, 'Who *are* you?'

'Callum Durand.'

'But there isn't a Callum Durand!' she exclaimed positively.

His long jeans-clad legs and booted feet had been making easy work of the tangled undergrowth, but he stopped dead and said mockingly, 'In that case, you're suspended in thin air.'

His arms loosened, Gaby felt herself dropping, and she clutched wildly at his white shirt. He laughed and caught her and began striding on. Gaby felt ruffled and foolish and she explained stiffly, 'I meant I've never *heard* of a Callum Durand. Justin doesn't have any cousins and he's an only son.'

'The only legitimate son,' he corrected her calmly. 'I'm his big brother—born, as they say in these quaint parts, on the wrong side of the blanket.'

'Good heavens!' Gaby breathed, her eyes widening.

'Yes,' he agreed, 'it was a bit of a shock all round.'

It seemed such a massive understatement to Gaby that she blinked wonderingly at him.

'Why do you keep doing that?' he asked.

Gaby was startled. 'What?'

'Blinking like an owl,' he told her softly.

'I don't blink like an owl!'

'Yes, you do. A soft, fluffy, very lovable little owl. It's——' he paused to select the right word with care '—beguiling. If you don't stop, I'm very much afraid I'm going to have to kiss you.'

She was so surprised that she blinked again, her thickly lashed lids sweeping down over her big brown eyes and then opening wider than ever.

'That does it,' Callum said.

Too late, Gaby read the intention in his eyes, which were no longer a flinty blue but glowing warmly. Her soft lips parted with dismay, not invitation, but it didn't make the slightest bit of difference. Callum's lips closed over hers with calm possession, for all the world as though he was claiming her as his own rather than in a conscious search for passion. It was all wrong, Gaby knew that, but still her senses reeled.

She didn't know how long he kissed her. It was too long and not long enough, and that, of course, was perfectly crazy. When he finally raised his head and studied her, he didn't look mocking or amused, just very grim, and she couldn't make any sense of that either.

Her brain felt fragmented, like a kaleidoscope which had been so violently shaken that the pieces were taking time to re-settle into a recognisable pattern. She could only think vaguely: It should have been Justin. No, that's wrong, I mean Harry. Oh, I don't know who it should have been, but not—not Callum Durand!

Gaby felt indignant and curiously upset. Having kissed her, he shouldn't be looking at her in that forbidding way as though it was all her fault. She found her breath and said bitterly, 'That was a liberty.'

'I did warn you.'

'Knowing very well I couldn't do anything about it,' she retorted. 'I don't know quite who you think you are, but becoming squire of Shorelands has gone to your head. You don't own this gatehouse and you don't own me.'

'It's only a matter of time,' he told her softly.

Gaby's eyes sparkled with wrath. 'If that's what you think, you don't know me! Now put me down and go away. You're the trespasser here.' When he made no move to do so, she went on with increased bitterness, 'I know I can't force you to! I can only ask, or isn't that enough? Does the squire want the gardener's grand-daughter to beg?'

She was set back on her feet and released so fast that she staggered and had to steady herself against the frame of the back porch. Callum reached around the side of it, pulled back the creeper and lifted a key from a hook. Gaby held out her left hand for it. He slapped it on her palm so violently that it fell to the ground before she could close her fingers over it. He didn't stop to retrieve it, but turned and strode away, a tall and broad figure so like Justin, and yet so unlike him.

No charm, no finesse, no caressing smiles. He was like a larger than life image of Justin, blown out of true so that flaws had crept in—and yet he shattered her in a way Justin never had. Justin appealed to her romantic soul, Callum to her earthier senses.

Gaby picked up the key and then sat down suddenly on one of the little benches on either side of the porch. Callum Durand, in just five minutes, had drained more out of her than her entire day's travelling. She was back at her beloved Shorelands, Justin was here, and yet she'd never felt so dejected in her entire life.

She found herself looking at her sore right hand.

Blood was oozing sluggishly from the bramble scratches, and there was a thorn embedded in her soft flesh. She tried ineffectually to get it out with her fingertips, wrapped her handkerchief round it, and, sighing for she knew not what, stood up to open the back door.

Gaby didn't know what to expect if there had been squatters here, but she could almost have wept with relief when she stepped into a neat and homely kitchen. She was, she knew, still being over-emotional, but after what she'd endured at Callum's hands she was grateful for any small mercies.

The cottage had a stale, closed-up smell. Gaby left the back door ajar, opened the kitchen window and walked through the living-room to open the front door. There was no hall or passage downstairs, each room opening on to the next. When the bathroom door was open and the fresh air circulating freely, she went back into the kitchen.

She was dying for a cup of tea, but her hand and leg were throbbing, demanding immediate attention. Gaby searched her handbag for a needle, tweezers, tissues and plaster, then looked hopefully in the sink cupboard. She was lucky, there was a bottle of disinfectant, just as there always used to be.

Within a few minutes she had her tights off and was standing barefoot on the flagged kitchen floor waiting for the kettle to boil. While the needle and tweezers were soaking in hot, disinfected water, she did a quick recce around the kitchen and found sugar and coffee in the walk-in pantry, which she supposed the cleaning woman must keep there.

Black coffee was better than nothing. Gaby made herself a cup and then set about extracting the thorn. It was a clumsy operation with her left hand. The thorn

was deep and it had gone in at an awkward angle. The
wound was sore enough, and she was only making it
worse. She was groaning with pain and vexation when
the room darkened.

She spun towards the door. Callum Durand stood
there, blocking out the sunlight. He ducked through
the low doorway, straightened up, caught his head a
glancing blow on an exposed beam and swore.

'Very pretty,' Gaby said, eying him with hostility.

'Sorry, but you fit this doll's house and I don't.'

'Nobody invited you in,' she retorted, wanting to
retreat as he came towards her, but pugnaciously
standing her ground. 'If you think being the squire
entitles you to——'

'Don't start that again,' Callum broke in, 'you'll only
make me mad.' He took her bloodied hand in his and
looked at it. 'So that's what the blood was about. I saw
it on my shirt, knew it wasn't mine, so I thought I'd
better come and check you're all right.'

'I'm fine, thank you, and I can manage perfectly well
on my own,' Gaby said with a frigid politeness that
swiftly broke down when she saw the sceptical look on
his face. She added waspishly, 'You're the trespasser
now, and, although I can't throw you out, I can soon
get somebody who can.'

Callum seemed amused. 'Who?'

'The police.'

'Now you're being silly.' He picked her up, sat her
on the kitchen counter as though she were indeed a
doll, and went on calmly, 'Sit still, shut up and I'll soon
have you fixed up.'

Words failed Gaby. There were so many things she
wanted to say—none of them flattering to Callum
Durand—that they jammed in her throat and she
couldn't say anything at all. He seemed satisfied,

because he left her to wash his hands at the sink, then took a clean teacloth from a drawer and wiped them.

'You seem to know your way around,' she said bitterly.

'I helped your cleaning lady straighten out the place after the squatters left.'

'*You* did? But why?' Gaby asked, surprised out of her hostility.

'Somebody had to. There were five of them, too many for these small rooms, and they'd shifted the furniture about.'

'I would have thought Sam Gibson——' she began.

'Ah, yes, your agent.' Callum made it sound as though he and Sam were not particular friends. 'Shall we say I happened to be here and he wasn't?'

Gaby had a feeling there was a lot he wasn't saying, and she was frowning over this when he came back to her. He took her hand again. It seemed very small in his big one and she said nervously, 'It's very sore.'

'Trust me,' Callum replied, 'and keep still.'

She couldn't think of any reason why she should trust him, but she didn't have any choice and fright kept her still. She really didn't fancy that needle going in her hand again, and to cover her fear she asked, 'When were the squatters here?'

'Last week. They were on their way south after a pop concert when they stumbled across this place.'

Callum was probing for the thorn with surprising gentleness, but Gaby, expecting to be hurt anyway, carried on talking nervously. 'How did you manage to get rid of five of them?' she asked.

'I threw out the biggest. The rest followed like lambs.'

Given Callum's size, that wasn't so hard to believe,

but she said dubiously, 'I thought squatters are protected by law. Shouldn't there have been some kind of court proceedings?'

'My way was quicker.'

'How very feudal,' Gaby murmured.

Callum paused and looked at her consideringly. The oddest feeling contracted Gaby's spine and pulsed through her veins. She wasn't afraid of him, so it couldn't be fear, and yet she felt threatened in some nameless way. Cravenly she told him, 'I'm very grateful, of course.'

'I don't want your gratitude.'

His blue eyes were still fixed on her, offering her a challenge she didn't understand. She was annoyed, and that gave her the courage to say, 'What do you want, then? I don't think you'd be bothering with me if you didn't want something.'

'When I make up my mind what it is, I'll let you know,' he replied, and began to probe her hand once more. Gaby yelped, but then he was holding up the thorn for her inspection.

Momentarily diverted, she exclaimed, 'Who'd have thought anything so small could cause so much trouble?'

Callum put his hands on the kitchen counter on either side of her and leaned towards her. 'I could say the same about you,' he murmured.

His face was very close to hers, his blue eyes gleaming in a way she'd seen before. For a dizzy moment she thought he was going to kiss her again, and for an even dizzier moment she wanted him to. Recollecting herself, she recoiled.

Callum frowned, then snapped, 'There's no need to play the vestal virgin. I try not to suffer a moment of madness more than once in any given day.' He stepped away from her, grasped her ankle and began to clean the scratches on her leg. 'You look like a pin-cushion,' he went on. 'What have you been doing with yourself?'

Gaby was flushing hotly and resisting the impulse to pull her skirt primly down over her knees, certain it would only invoke another of his caustic remarks. In some contrary way she preferred to feel threatened to foolish, and she seized the change of subject gratefully, explaining, 'I got my foot caught in some briars in the garden and fell on them.'

'Hmm.' Gaby was wondering what that 'hmm' meant when he continued, 'I'll send a man over tomorrow to get the garden cleared. It was the state of it that let the squatters know the gatehouse was empty.'

Gaby was tiring of his autocratic ways, and she replied stiffly, 'Thank you, but I prefer to make my own arrangements.'

'Suit yourself.' Callum dried her leg with a clean tissue. Suddenly he seemed brisk, as if he was tiring of her, too. 'These scratches are superficial and best left as they are. You'll need a plaster on your hand until it's healed over.'

He held out his own hand peremptorily, and sulkily Gaby slapped a plaster in it. She was piqued by his loss of interest, although not for the life of her could she have said why. His dark head was bent close to hers while he fixed the plaster on her hand, and she felt the wildest urge to reach out and touch his hair. Only because it was like Justin's, she told herself, not too convincingly.

'Are you covered for tetanus?' Callum asked abruptly.

'I had a booster last month. I cut my hand on a tin.'

'You're not safe to let loose on your own, are you?' He finished sticking on the plaster and let go of her hand. 'Haven't you got a boyfriend to take care of you?'

Gaby could feel her anger rekindling and she retorted, 'Boys don't interest me. I have a *man* friend, if that's what you mean, and I can take very good care of myself.'

'You could have fooled me,' Callum replied derisively, then changed tack. 'You're some kind of office temp, aren't you? What's this man friend of yours doing, letting you run loose in the country by yourself? You'll probably have a nervous breakdown at the things that go bump in the night. Old places creak a lot, you know.'

'If I can survive the hazards of the day,' she told him scathingly, searing him with a look that left him in no doubt she was referring to him, 'the nights aren't likely to hold any terrors for me.'

His big hand came under her chin, forcing her face up to his. 'Be very careful, Gaby,' he said threateningly. 'Don't tempt me to show you how much of a hazard I can really be.'

Gaby pushed his hand away contemptuously. 'Don't play the squire with me, Callum Durand. You're a pseud, and I'm used to the real thing.'

They were brave words, but when Gaby saw the flame flicker in his eyes she wished she'd held her tongue. Callum yanked her roughly from the kitchen counter and clamped her against his lean, hard body. She was shocked, her heart pounding with primitive fear and then surging with an equally primitive excitement.

His hand caught in her hair, twisted it painfully so that her face was jerked up to his, and his mouth came down savagely to cover hers. Gaby tried to fight, but the flame she'd seen in his eyes seemed to flicker through her body, igniting her in a way she'd never known before.

Where she'd been straining away from him, she found herself straining towards him. She felt his hands move possessively down her back and roam round to explore her firm young breasts. Gaby gasped as her nipples hardened and Callum teased them into an aching, unbearable yearning.

She pressed her breasts against his experienced hands in an unavailing attempt to quench the desire he aroused in her, her own hands beginning a wild and urgent exploration of his back, kneading the muscles and moving up to his broad shoulders.

Suddenly—so suddenly that her trembling legs almost collapsed with shock—he thrust her away from him. She stared at him dazedly, not understanding. The flame was still in his eyes, but this time it flickered out to her with the heat of fury and the ice of scorn. 'You made it plain enough what you think of the squire,' he told her with savage satisfaction, 'but you've made it plainer still what you think of the man. Now what have you got to say for yourself, little Gaby Warren?'

Gaby understood then. His passion had been nothing but simulation, a deliberate exercise in mastery which she, to her undying shame, had been unable to deny. Her huge eyes dulled with an inexpressible pain. She felt sick, actually physically sick. The flush of desire faded from her cheeks, leaving her with an unearthly pallor. She felt used, abused, unclean.

From somewhere deep within her the rage of humiliation came to her aid. She stepped back and dealt him a stinging blow across his cheek. He didn't try to avoid it. Perhaps there was some scrap of fairness within himself that made him feel he deserved it.

Gaby didn't know and couldn't begin to guess. She turned away, disgusted. When she looked again he was gone. She leaned against the kitchen counter and dropped her tousled head in her trembling hands, eyes pressed tight against tears she was too proud to shed.

She was waiting for sanity to return. It was a painful process and it took time. It was also confusing and frightening. Because, dimly at first, and then with growing clarity she began to perceive what had really happened to her, and it knocked her known world sideways.

She'd returned to Shorelands to make her peace with Justin's memory so that she could marry Harry, but all she'd done was fall foul of a man who had the power to obliterate them both from her mind and senses. Where on earth did she go from here?

CHAPTER FOUR

THE night brought Gaby some kind of counsel, but very little peace of mind. She could only suppose that Callum had in some weird way triggered off her suppressed longing for Justin. It was her mistake, her humiliation, and she'd just have to learn to live with it.

Callum was a brute and, she told herself contemptuously, more than a bit pathetic. He was the bastard son who'd somehow got hold of Shorelands and was overplaying the role of squire because he hadn't been bred to it the way Justin had. He must be aware of his own inadequacy, poor man, which was why he reacted so harshly to criticism.

Gaby, pitying Callum because it was easier than pitying herself, managed to soothe herself enough to fall asleep. It wasn't very hard to be defiant while she was tucked up safely in bed in the pretty little primrose room she'd always used, but when she awoke to the first rays of the rising sun slanting through the leaded diamond panes of her lattice window she didn't feel half as tough.

The comfort of the night was gone and here was the day, and there was no guessing what it might hold for her. Gaby felt unprepared, vulnerable. The gatehouse was securely locked, but her eyes went instinctively to the door, half expecting Callum to come crashing through it.

She was being ridiculous and she knew it, but such was the power of the man and the force of the impression he'd made on her that she got out of bed and dressed rapidly in jeans and a floppy loose-knit jumper. She ran lightly down the stairs, feeling more normal, more like herself, now that she was up and about.

Gaby pottered around the kitchen for a few minutes, making herself tea and toast, trying to concentrate on planning her day. It wasn't easy, because her mind was full of things she didn't want to think about. Harry was one. He seemed very remote now, but she supposed that was reasonable enough because he'd never been a part of her life here at Shorelands. Justin was another. She felt confused about him as well. He'd promised they'd get better acquainted, but he must have returned to the manor house through the main gates because he hadn't come by here. And there was Callum. No, she definitely didn't want to think about Callum.

A glance at her watch revealed it wasn't even six o'clock yet. It would be hours before she could visit Sam Gibson to find out what had been going on at Shorelands. So what? she asked herself with mock jauntiness. There was plenty to do around here. The garden, for one thing. She'd meant to hire a jobbing gardener, but she was full of restless energy and it seemed a good idea to make a start herself.

She was a Warren, she knew a flower from a weed. Her grandfather had made sure her long summer holidays hadn't been spent entirely on mooning over Justin. There was a shed full of tools, and when she looked inside she saw her tenants hadn't been as tidy as Grandad, but she found a scythe, shears and clippers, and her wellingtons and heavy-duty gloves were still there.

Gaby set about clearing the paths so that she could walk around the garden without danger to life and limb, trundling wheelbarrow loads of nettles and brambles to what had once been the vegetable patch, where they could be burned when they dried out.

She became engrossed in her work, finding a kind of happiness in slashing and hacking away as though there were no tomorrow, and was amazed when next she looked at her watch to find it was getting on for ten o'clock. The sun was hot now, the early morning dew was all steamed away, and she'd long since discarded her jumper for a light T-shirt.

Her muscles, unused to hard physical work, ached a little as she straightened up, but Gaby was pleased with her efforts. A few more hours of this and she could progress to rediscovering Grandad's once beautiful flower-beds. More importantly, she felt as though she'd rediscovered herself. Somehow she'd sweated away the humiliation and the hold Callum seemed to have over her.

She no longer felt frail and defenceless, but cheerful and confident. The feudal aura of Shorelands might have got to Callum Durand, but it wouldn't get to her again. She would be able to cope with him if he strayed her way again. He'd caught her on the hop, that was all, vulnerable after seeing Justin again after so long.

Callum, with supreme arrogance, had made up his mind that she was a silly little bimbo he could treat as he wanted. She was tempted to string him along before letting him know what a mistake he'd made. He might be less inclined to mock others if he was mocked himself. It was a thought to cheer herself up with, anyway.

An hour later, bathed, perfumed and with her usual self-confidence restored, Gaby was driving towards Shevingham. She was wearing a navy-blue shantung frock with narrow pleats falling from a dropped waist-line. The little sleeves were primly edged with white, but the wide white sailor collar plunged deeply enough to reveal the provocative swell of her breasts.

The sides of her rich brown hair were tied with a navy-blue bow at the back of her head and the rest fell freely to below her shoulders. Glossy pink lipstick moistened her lips, her skin was a little sun-kissed from her work in the garden and there was a martial gleam in her eye.

Gaby didn't know whether she would come across Justin or Callum, but she was ready for either—Justin because he hadn't exactly fallen over himself to see her again as he'd promised, and Callum because. . .well, it was best not to think about Callum. She'd only get mad again.

But her spirits continued to rise. For one thing, the day had kept its early promise. For another, the Durand brothers were mortal men, not the gods they seemed to think themselves, and she was a woman. Whatever happened, she intended to strike a few sparks off both of them while she was at Shorelands.

When she strolled into Sam Gibson's office he raised his head, a business smile already pinned on his mouth. The smile froze while he stared at her, then widened. 'Gaby Warren, by all that's wonderful!' he exclaimed, coming round his desk with outstretched arms. He gave her a big hug and then stood back, studying her. 'I don't know whether to scold or kiss you. First you're a year late and now you're a month early.'

Gaby laughed, thinking he'd put on a little weight since last she'd seen him. He was a handsome young man, though, with curly brown hair, hazel eyes and a smart moustache over his still smiling lips. 'Sorry about last summer,' she apologised, 'but as I wrote and told you, I went to Italy instead.'

'You also wrote that you'd be back this September, and here you are at the beginning of August. Are you always so unpredictable, Gaby? Not that you're not welcome at any time, of course,' Sam said with another smile. He steered her to the chair in front of his desk and then sat down in his own.

'I managed to wangle some extra time.' She looked across the desk at him and said bluntly, 'What's been going on at Shorelands? I was treated like a trespasser last night by somebody who called himself Callum Durand.'

'Ah. . .the bastard squire,' he murmured.

'Sam!'

He shrugged. 'That's what we call him around here. He's a Durand all right—you can see that just by looking at him—but as he's illegitimate he doesn't have any right to use the name.'

'Then why does he?' Gaby asked.

'I don't know, and he's not the sort of bloke you can ask awkward questions. We reckon he's suffering from delusions of grandeur. He certainly knows how to throw his weight about, and he comes down heavily on anybody who stands in his way. I'd steer clear of him if I were you, Gaby. He's not a very savoury character. He's taking everything that he can from Justin. I suppose in some twisted way he thinks it should have been his—if he'd been legitimate, that is.'

Gaby's curved eyebrows puckered. 'You mean Shorelands?'

'That was the start. Now he's after Justin's girl.'

'His—his girl?' Gaby silently cursed her slight stutter, and covered it by joking, 'Are we talking about the same Justin Durand? I thought he never narrowed it down to less than a dozen at any one time.'

Sam grinned. 'I know what you mean, but Kate Armstrong's a stayer. They've been a regular twosome on and off for years. Did you ever meet the Armstrongs up at Shevingham Hall?'

'No, I was never in that league,' Gaby replied flippantly, although Kate had been around Shorelands so much she'd have had to have been blind not to have seen her. Kate was a striking redhead a few years older than herself, and Gaby had envied her deeply. She'd been part of Justin's charmed circle, always riding, driving or playing tennis with him. For a fleeting second Gaby felt like a waif again, very much the gardener's granddaughter on the outside looking in.

She pulled herself together and said, 'Sam, I'm as much at sea as ever. You're assuming I know much more than I do. It's four years since I've been at Shorelands. Justin was in the States then. How long has he been back, and when did this brother of his turn up?'

'Sorry. Callum Durand's been so much *the* topic of conversation around here that it's easy to assume everybody knows the ins and outs of it——' Sam broke off to turn to his secretary, a pretty freckle-faced blonde who had been working diligently at a word processor on the other side of the room. 'Amanda, be a love and make some coffee, will you? Oh, just remembered you two haven't met! Gaby Warren— Amanda Highfield.'

The two girls smiled at each other, and then Amanda left the room. Sam continued, 'Justin was in New York for four years learning the publishing business with some sort of relation of his mother's, then he came back and set up his own company.'

Four years ago, Gaby thought. We must have just missed each other. Aloud she asked, because she had to, 'Did he return to Shorelands?'

'No. He's often at Shevingham Hall with the Armstrongs, though. We all expected him to marry Kate when he's ready to settle down, but now it looks as though Callum might,' Sam went on. 'She's done well, has our Kate. She's a stockbroker. She has the right family background, but it's still quite an achievement. She's become the sort of female power figure some men find irresistible.'

His tone implied that he didn't, but Gaby said nothing, anxious to hear more. 'She met Callum Durand by chance at some City function or other. He's a venture capitalist—that's somebody who pumps money into a promising business, puts in a good management team and sells out when the profits are high enough,' Sam explained.

Gaby, who could have given him a far more detailed definition of a venture capitalist, just nodded meekly and prompted, 'What happened then?'

'The inevitable, although it was damn bad timing.' Sam didn't explain what he meant, but pushed on, 'Callum's name, his looks. . .Kate would have had to be dumb not to put two and two together, and she's as smart as they come. Naturally she asked what sort of a relation he was to Justin and whether he'd ever been to Shorelands. Callum claimed he'd never heard of either. He must have been lying, otherwise he wouldn't be using the Durand name, would he? He's a self-made man so he wasn't always rich. Justin reckons he adopted the family name and background to give him credibility when he was starting out. In other words, he's a pseud whose chance meeting with Kate forced him into backing up his claims.'

Gaby remembered calling Callum a pseud herself, and shivered not altogether unpleasurably when she remembered his reaction. She looked down, afraid that something of what she was feeling was showing in her lamentably expressive eyes, and asked, 'Who told you all this?'

'Justin. He got it from Kate. She introduced them and brought Callum up to see Shorelands. She didn't realise at the time that it was the worst possible turn she could have served Justin.'

'Why?' Gaby asked, then found Amanda at her side offering her a cup of coffee. 'Thanks,' she said. Her eyebrows rose questioningly as she surprised a strained look on Amanda's face, but before she could say anything Amanda gave Sam his coffee and hurriedly returned to her desk as he began to speak again.

'The Hazletts had just put Shorelands on the market. As she got older and less active, Mrs Hazlett found life too bleak up here, especially in winter. She wanted to return to Devon where most of her family and friends are. Justin couldn't afford to buy Shorelands by himself, so he set up a consortium. He was the principal shareholder with a few local businessmen, myself included, chipping in. The idea was to turn the manor into a health farm. It would have made a bomb!'

Gaby, sipping her coffee, found she didn't like the idea of Shorelands being commercialised, but her grandfather's heart had broken because he hadn't been able to change with the times, and she'd no intention of going the same way. Still, she was relieved that it hadn't happened, even if that did seem disloyal to Justin. 'I gather Callum outbid Justin,' she said.

'You've got it in one.'

'But there's not too much resentment between them?

I mean, Justin's staying at Shorelands, isn't he?' she asked.

'For a few days here and there. He has to keep in with Callum or leave him a clear field with Kate. She comes up from London every weekend.'

'So that's how it is. Still, Callum wouldn't invite him if there was bad blood between them, would he?' Gaby pointed out.

'I suppose it boosts his ego to play host to his legitimate brother in the ancestral home. It certainly amuses him to play the squire.'

The hostility she'd noticed in Callum's voice when Sam had been mentioned was there in Sam's as well now. Gaby wondered about that, then commented, 'There doesn't seem to be much love lost between you and Callum.'

'There isn't,' Sam agreed. 'Justin's a good friend of mine, and we'd have made a lot of money if Callum hadn't meddled. To be honest, we were both flamingly angry and we thought, if Callum wanted Shorelands so much, why didn't we put in a higher bid? We couldn't have met it, of course, but Callum wasn't to know that. He had to outbid us again, so, although he got Shorelands anyway, he was bled for it. Unfortunately, he got wind of what we'd done—God knows how!—and blames me for it. Justin escaped his wrath, presumably because Callum gets his kicks by lording it over him. I suppose being a bastard makes one a bit malicious.'

An innate sense of fairness made Gaby say, 'You and Justin weren't above a bit of malice yourself, were you?'

Sam smiled. 'It's a cruel world, Gaby, and we local boys have to take care of ourselves as best we can. Whose side are you on, anyway?'

'Nobody's,' she replied slowly, needing time to consider what she'd learned about both the Durands. 'I'm here for a holiday, not a feud.'

'And to sell the cottage,' Sam reminded her. 'It's going to be a pleasure dealing with Callum on your behalf.'

'Callum? What makes you think he wants to buy?' Gaby asked, but even as she did so she recalled his saying his not owning the gatehouse was 'only a matter of time'.

'Because it once belonged to the Durands. That makes it irresistible to him. He's got to own it all, every last ancestral inch.'

'What makes you so sure of that?' Gaby was beginning to think that Sam was so disgruntled over the failure of the consortium to get Shorelands that it was colouring his whole attitude towards Callum. Her own attitude to him wasn't exactly sweetness and light, but fair was fair.

Sam began fiddling with a pen. A sign, she wondered, of unease? He sounded confident enough, though, when he replied, 'Do you remember the two farms, Mallows and Lower Mead, that were sold separately when the estate was broken up? The consortium was negotiating for those as well, but the same thing happened again and Callum snaffled them. He wants the gatehouse, all right, and he'll have to deal with me to get it. He won't like that at all.'

Gaby didn't like the feeling that she was being caught up in petty feuding that had nothing to do with her, nor did she relish being a pawn in the game. Something else held her back as well. Justin was back at Shorelands. He might be after Kate, but nothing was settled, least of all the yearnings of her romantic heart.

'Hang on,' she said slowly. 'I know selling the cottage

is practical because I'm never going to live there myself, but I've just got back and I'm not feeling too practical at the moment. Give me a couple of weeks for the novelty to wear off and boredom to set in, then we'll talk business, all right?'

Sam considered her in a carefully assessing way that reminded her irresistibly of Harry, and for some reason she frowned. Sam saw the frown and his own face lightened. 'Why not?' he said easily. 'The longer Callum's kept in doubt of your intentions, the higher I'll be able to push the price.'

'I don't want extortion,' Gaby told him quickly. 'Just a fair market price.'

'A fair market price, love, is what somebody is prepared to pay, but you don't have to worry your pretty little head about that. Leave it all to me.'

Somebody else who thinks I'm a bimbo, Gaby thought disgruntledly, but she let it pass. Sam could be sorted out any time, and she had bigger fish to fry. She put her cup and saucer down on his desk and said, 'I need a new set of keys. Callum told me about the squatters and the locks have been changed. He showed me where the back door key's kept, but I'd prefer to hide that somewhere else now in case I lock myself out.'

'The way Callum turfed out those squatters was just one example of his high-handedness. He should have called me in to deal with them,' Sam replied bitterly, then turned his head to his secretary. 'A set of keys for the gatehouse, please.'

Amanda unlocked a drawer and brought over three keys on a ring. 'The small ones are for the front and back doors and the big one's for the door in the gates,' she explained.

'Thanks.' Gaby dropped the keys in her handbag

and, when Amanda had gone back to her desk, she said to Sam, 'High-handed or not, Callum did me a favour. If the squatters were still there I'd be in a bit of a pickle, wouldn't I?'

'You mean you like the man?' Sam asked.

'No, I don't, but that doesn't bother me because I don't expect I'll see much of him. He doesn't exactly like me, either.' She didn't want Sam to enquire quite how she'd fallen foul of Callum, so she asked, 'How come he found out about the squatters before you?'

'I'd hired Mrs Foley, who also chars at the manor, to keep the cottage clean. She discovered them and went straight to Callum instead of me. I fired her.'

'That was a bit rough!' Gaby exclaimed. 'She probably only did what she thought was best.'

'I didn't want a spy in the camp. She's in and out of this office a lot because she cleans other cottages I hire out for their owners. I think she must have seen or heard something about the consortium's pushing up the price of Shorelands, and tipped Callum off.'

'That's only supposition, surely?' Gaby protested.

'Is it? Then why has she got a permanent job at the manor and a flat to go with it? It's Callum and his squire syndrome again, distributing largess among his trusty servitors. Come to think of it, he probably wants your gatehouse for her. She's got two young children and he can't want them under his feet. Packing them off to the gatehouse would solve the problem nicely. Do you want me to get you another char?'

Gaby considered for a moment, then said, 'No, thanks. I'm no lover of housework, but the place is as neat as a pin and it shouldn't be too much hassle to keep it that way. There's no guarantee another char will be as conscientious as Mrs Foley.'

'Cunning, more like.'

'You are bitter,' Gaby murmured.

'Are you surprised? If the consortium had got Shorelands I'd have been set up for life.'

'Oh, come on,' Gaby mocked. 'A health farm wouldn't exactly have made millions, would it?'

Sam began drumming his pen against the desk, a distinctly irritable sound. 'It would have been a nice steady earner,' he replied eventually.

He really had taken it hard, and to try and cheer him up she said lightly, '*C'est la vie*. . .'

'That might be what you say in Paris, but you've been abroad too long, Gaby. We're a bit more pithy around here,' Sam snapped. He saw the way her eyebrows drew together, and instantly his smile was back. He went on with his usual breeziness, 'Let's forget about it, unless there's anything else you want to know about our precious squire?'

'Well, I must admit I find the situation intriguing,' Gaby admitted. 'How long has he owned Shorelands?'

'Three months. At first he came up just at the weekends, but now he's here most of the time. He makes two or three trips to London a week, and that's about it. He's filled the old estate manager's office with computers and is mostly operating from there. I told you, he's really into this squire lark—far more than Justin ever was, and he was born to it. A venture capitalist tramping around the meadows and fussing over the marshes—it's ludicrous! I wonder what old man Durand would say if he was still alive.' Sam stopped and a reminiscent gleam came into his eyes. 'Damn Callum to hell and back, if I know old Crispin. After all, he never did acknowledge Callum as his own.'

'I didn't know Justin's father—I mean, *their* father—had died,' Gaby said.

'Two years ago,' Sam told her, 'so he can't confirm or deny anything. Callum's mother's dead, so it all comes back to his likeness to Justin and his appropriation of the family name. According to Justin, Callum says he has letters from Crispin Durand to his mother proving his paternity, but he's never shown them, and if he's telling the truth he must have known about Shorelands before Kate told him about it, and why should he lie about that? Nothing about the man quite adds up.' Sam shrugged, then complained, 'It was just such appalling luck, Callum's turning up just as Justin was about to get Shorelands back.'

Gaby didn't reply immediately, but she could understand why Callum was such a hot topic of conversation. Nobody knew anything about him for certain, and gossip couldn't have a better breeding ground, especially with Sam's animosity fuelling it. One of his phrases stuck in her mind, and she asked, 'What did you mean about Callum fussing over the marshes?'

'Did I say that? I meant just fussing generally. The man's a born meddler.'

Gaby stood up and smiled. 'I never expected such heavy vibes to be hanging over Shorelands. I've always thought of it as a place of peace and tranquillity. Oh, well, so long as the ghosts of past Durands don't rise up against the illegitimate usurper, I suppose the situation will sort itself out.'

Sam grinned, but again Gaby's sense of fairness troubled her. She'd talked to Sam too long. She was getting spiteful, too. 'Not that Callum is a usurper,' she corrected quickly. 'He bought Shorelands fair and square.'

'Thereby denying Justin the chance to get back his ancestral home,' Sam pointed out.

'There is that,' Gaby acknowledged, but as she had

more than enough to think about already she said her goodbyes and left. She stood by her car, deep in thought.

Justin, Kate and Callum. What an explosive triangle. Were the brothers pursuing Kate out of love—or rivalry? And Kate—was she flirting with Callum to bring Justin to heel at last, or had she decided Callum was the better bet? Callum had money and power, Justin charm and breeding. Would a successful businesswoman like Kate follow her mind or her heart?

Gaby knew what she would do, but she also knew that her heart was wilful and not to be trusted. It whispered things to her that she shouldn't listen to, and what it was whispering now was that the love triangle was viable, uncommitted. There was room for somebody else to move in, if that somebody else cared enough. . .

Gaby shook her head, as if to clear her clouded brain. Shorelands was getting at her again, making her fanciful, romantic. There was something about the place that made the impossible seem possible, although nobody knew better than she what an illusion that was. Justin had never been anything more than a foolish dream, much better to let him stay that way. Harry was reality. Harry was her future.

She waited for her heart to whisper the opposite, but for once it was silent—as confused, it seemed, as she was. Losing patience with herself, she decided to go straight back into Sam's office and put the gatehouse up for sale immediately. Instinct told her it was the only safe, the only sane thing to do.

She stepped resolutely away from her car and cannoned into a passer-by. She was caught, steadied and abruptly released. She stepped back and the instinctive words of apology she was about to utter died stillborn.

She was looking up at Callum Durand, big, bronzed and strangely threatening in tight jeans and with the sleeves of his denim shirt rolled up to reveal his muscular arms. The collar was unbuttoned, too, and she saw hair as dark as that on his head curling up to his strong throat.

Gaby was furious with herself for being silly enough to feel threatened in a busy, sunny high street, and even more furious that his visual impact jolted her as much as the actual collision. She said rudely, 'Oh, it's you. You seem to be making a habit of getting in my way.'

'I could say the same about you.' Callum was inspecting her as thoroughly as he had last night and then his eyes went to the estate agents' office where she was clearly heading. His hand went under her elbow, turning her aside and steering her along the street to the Fisherman's Dream. He cut short her indignant protests by telling her, 'Gibson's a shark. If you're selling the gatehouse, deal directly with me and save yourself his commission.'

'Sam's a friend of mine,' Gaby retorted. 'He has my best interests at heart.'

'Try to use whatever brains you were born with. Gibson's only ever interested in lining his own pockets. Take a leaf out of his book and you'll save yourself a lot of money,' Callum told her in the same tone he'd have used to teach a child the alphabet. 'It makes sense, you know it does. All you need is an independent valuation so you can be certain of fair play. We'll talk about it over coffee.'

Gaby found herself thrust willy-nilly into the lounge bar of the Fisherman's Dream. She pulled herself free of him and said fiercely, 'You're overplaying the squire bit again, Callum Durand. Let me tell you——'

She got no further. A man dressed impeccably in beautifully cut cavalry twill trousers, with a silk cravat filling the open collar of his light green shirt, straightened up from the bar at the sound of her voice. He glanced round, flashed the brilliant smile that had haunted Gaby's dreams, and put down his glass.

'Gaby, by all that's wonderful,' he murmured, strolling towards her. 'I was wondering what would happen to liven a damnably boring day. Ah, I see you've met my——' he paused fractionally but significantly before adding '——brother.'

'Justin,' Gaby breathed. She realised she'd put more significance into his name than she should have, and hurried on, 'Yes, Callum and I have met—after a fashion. He seems to think I'm selling the gatehouse, and I was just about to explain I haven't made up my mind what to do with it yet. We have this problem, your. . .brother. . .and I. I don't get a chance to talk and he doesn't want to listen anyway.'

Callum took her sarcasm in silence, but Justin laughed. 'We have the same problem, but before we talk about that I must tell you how cute you are. You look as though you've fallen out of a Victorian seaside photograph. Enchanting.'

Enchanting. . . Harry's word, that Justin was making his own. Gaby smiled, knowing that her sailor frock was reminiscent of a bygone era, but more because his flattery was balm to her wounded dignity. 'A pity I left my bucket and spade at home,' she teased.

'We can soon remedy that.' Justin's arm went around her shoulders and he steered her towards the bar. 'Come and have a drink, then we'll take a stroll along the beach and catch up on old times.'

Gaby was sorely tempted, but for some peculiar reason Callum's silence and his critical eyes made her

feel uncomfortable. Pride, too, held her back. She
didn't want to fall too readily into Justin's arms. Justin
was a hunter. He must be, or he'd have married years
ago. She mustn't be too available.

'Another time,' she said. 'I have a lot of things to do
today.' She avoided looking at Callum, and went on, 'I
only called in to leave a message at the bar.'

'What can I do to make you change your mind?'
Justin coaxed. 'Do old times mean nothing to you?'

'We don't have any,' Gaby protested laughingly. 'It's
eight years since we were both at Shorelands at the
same time, and I was only fourteen years old!'

'But you adored me then. Why else all the lurking
and spying?' Justin teased.

Gaby blushed—all the more fiercely because Callum
was there. Damn the man, she thought. If it were only
Justin and me, I'd be enjoying myself. Feeling pretty
stupid, she decided she could only bluff it through by
teasing as hard as Justin. 'Ah, those were the days,'
she said, managing a reminiscent sigh. 'You were my
knight in shining armour and you could do no wrong.
What a shame it had to pass, but those things do, you
know, like measles and mumps.'

Justin looked taken aback, then he laughed. 'Very
good, Gaby! You do realise that sounds suspiciously
like a challenge?'

'Phooey! I'm not issuing any challenges——' her
eyes flickered to Callum '—nor accepting any, either.'
His eyes had that flinty look again, and she was
disconcerted enough to wonder how long she could
keep this up. To her relief, the publican, John Harding,
walked through from the saloon bar and she went
towards him gratefully, saying, 'Mr Harding, it's been
four years, but do you remember me?'

'Gaby!' John Harding didn't need a second glance

before his seamed and weatherbeaten face lit up. He'd bought the pub when he left the Merchant Navy fifteen years before, and now he was close to retirement age. The salt-and-pepper hair and beard Gaby remembered were iron-grey. He seemed smaller, too, definitely more frail, but his movements were still brisk.

He raised the flap in the counter and came out purposefully to give her a big hug. 'It's good to have you back, Gaby. It has been a long time, but I still miss seeing your grandfather sitting in his favourite corner of the public bar with his nightly pint of local-brewed.'

'The gatehouse isn't the same without him, either. I knew it wouldn't be. That's why I stayed away so long.' Gaby was fibbing for pride's sake. She could scarcely give her real reason, with Justin so close and Callum breathing down her neck. They weren't to know she and Grandad had had little point of contact beyond kinship. He'd been too wrapped up in the past, and she in vivid dreams of a future with Justin.

It was a shame, but it was too late to do anything about it now. Suddenly Gaby felt more lost, more orphaned than she'd felt for years. Nothing could be more ridiculous. She had Harry now, a super job and lots of friends. Loneliness couldn't possibly penetrate such a barrier, particularly as she was capable of passing whatever solitary hours she had in a happy dream world.

But somehow, since returning to Shorelands, she seemed to have lost the ability to dream. The secret whisper in her heart was silent. Was it because Justin was a real living, breathing man again or. . . Wonderingly, Gaby turned her head to look at Callum.

Perhaps he read the bewilderment in her eyes, because he frowned. That frown, in some peculiar way, hurt Gaby. She felt as though somebody had shifted the very touchstones of her life, and she no longer knew what she was doing or why, or even who she was.

Something within her was changing. She didn't want it to, but she couldn't stop it. Too late, she realised she should never have come back to Shorelands. She hadn't so much stepped out of a dream as into a nightmare.

CHAPTER FIVE

GABY tore her eyes away from Callum, and found John Harding smiling at her in such a pleasantly uncomplicated way that her spinning head steadied. 'Are you back for good?' he asked.

'Chance would be a fine thing,' she responded, laughing. 'I have to earn my living and there's no work for me around here. That's why I took off in the first place.'

John pursed his lips. 'The gatehouse must be worth a pretty penny if you're hard up.'

'Oh, it might not come to that.' Gaby was determined to keep Callum guessing. Not because of anything Sam Gibson had said, but because of the cavalier way in which Callum treated her. 'John, can I ask a favour? There's no phone at the gatehouse, and I wondered if you'd take any messages for me. I'll drop by every day to see if anybody's trying to get in touch.'

'Consider it done!' John gave her a meaningful look and asked, 'Anybody special?'

'*Very*.' Gaby put a lot of emphasis in the word, thinking it wouldn't do Justin any harm to know she wasn't entirely on the loose.

'I'm surprised you haven't been snapped up before now,' John said.

Gaby's lips curved into an impish smile. 'I'm very fussy,' she explained.

Justin's arm slipped around her waist. 'So am I. Maybe we're a natural pair.'

Gaby laughed and twisted out of his grip. 'Who are

you kidding? The way you flirt, you can't take much pleasing.'

'Cat,' Justin said appreciatively. 'I can be serious. Try me.'

Gaby, who'd been dreaming for years of an invitation like this, now found that she couldn't accept it. With Callum and John listening, she had too much pride to fall so easily into his arms. 'No thanks, Justin. I don't care to get lost in the crush.'

John laughed and Justin's eyes gleamed in a predatory way. Why was Callum so silent? He wasn't the sort of man easily pushed into the background. But Justin was saying, 'So the cat has claws. How interesting. . . Callum, invite her to your dinner party this evening. She's just what we need to liven things up. It might amuse you to entertain a load of local bigwigs, but it won't amuse me.'

Callum, though, refused to endorse the invitation, telling Justin, 'You can always drop out if you think it's going to be that bad.'

Gaby could only be glad that John was called away by the pinging of the service bell in the other bar. Justin's smouldering eyes told her he considered himself as snubbed as she was, and she said hastily, 'Thanks for the thought, Justin, but I shouldn't think it's my sort of thing, either. Well, I must dash. I have lots of things to catch up on this morning.'

She left a heavy silence behind her heralding, she suspected, an almighty quarrel. It was true she'd meant to strike sparks off the Durand brothers, but individually. She hadn't meant to put them at each other's throats. Perhaps with her out of the way it would all blow over.

Gaby, unable to stop smarting because Callum didn't want her at his dinner party, could still see faults on both sides. Justin hadn't had the right to invite her, but Callum could have found a more tactful way of getting the message across. It rather seemed as though Sam Gibson was right, and Callum enjoyed lording it over Justin.

She was so preoccupied as she shopped, throwing items at random into her trolley, that she ended up with far more groceries than she needed. Back at the gatehouse she stacked everything away, had a sandwich and a glass of milk, then changed her clothes and returned to the garden.

Hard work had been a useful therapy that morning, and she was in need of more this afternoon. A new dimension had been added to her problem. It had been bad enough with her mind wanting Harry and her heart yearning for Justin. Now her body was reacting much too positively to Callum. She was so self-conscious when he was close to her, so uneasy, and yet so stimulated in an uncomfortable sort of way. He made her feel as though she were living on the edge, just a hair's breadth away from some unimaginable disaster. Nothing else could explain the adrenalin that surged through her like a forbidden drug. She felt a fresh flutter of nervous excitement just thinking about him.

But still the secret whisper in her heart remained silent, refusing to beguile or advise her. She was on her own, having to make rational judgements in an increasingly irrational situation. With something like despair she wondered whether she'd been wiser at fourteen than she was at twenty-two. At least she'd known what she wanted then. She hadn't suffered from this sort of confusion.

All she could be certain of now was that Harry in his own good time would marry her. Justin would certainly flirt with her. As for Callum, he wanted nothing from

her but the gatehouse. Perhaps that was what made
him so damnably attractive. She wasn't into power and
riches, but she was feminine enough to suffer from
pique.

Gaby, scything with more vigour than competence
the mini-meadow that had once been the lawn, paused
to allow a butterfly to escape. Its flight was slow, lazy,
as though it couldn't believe it had anything to fear in
this sun-drowsy garden, and it came to rest not far
away, where she would have to disturb it again soon.

'It's all right for some. . .' Gaby murmured, bending
to her work again and quite forgetting that all this
gardening was a self-inflicted chore. She straightened
again almost immediately. A car was approaching from
the manor. Justin or Callum?

She cast a swift look down at herself, uncertain
whether to flee to smarten herself up. The battered
straw hat, retrieved from the shed, that she was using
to shade her face and keep her hair off her neck had
seen better days, and her wellingtons certainly looked
incongruous with her scarlet shorts and brief halter
top.

She wasn't fit to be seen by either of them, but a
cantankerous streak in her nature made her stand her
ground. She couldn't transform herself into bandbox
perfection at the slightest hint of a Durand approaching. She'd be a nervous wreck, and it would be all too
obvious, anyway. Country people weren't smart, particularly when they were rediscovering gardens.

The gatehouse and its garden were an open oasis in
a band of trees that edged the outer walls of
Shorelands. It was broken only by the driveway, so she
wouldn't see the car until it was level with her low
garden wall, but somehow she didn't think it would be
Justin. She still associated him with the throaty roar of

a wicked-looking sports car, and this was something entirely different.

Callum, then, she thought—and wished she'd fled.

Gaby honestly didn't know whether she was relieved or disappointed when a blue Mini drew up and the plump figure of Mrs Hoskins, the manor's house-keeper, got out. She was carrying a wicker basket and Gaby clumped towards her as she came up the newly cleared path.

'Gaby, my dear!' Mrs Hoskins exclaimed, bending to kiss Gaby's hot cheek. 'Mr Justin told me you were back last night, and I've been trying all day to snatch a moment to get over to see you. Mr Callum's giving a dinner party tonight so things have been a bit fraught.'

Mr Justin and Mr Callum, Gaby thought. How archaic. Were the peasants still expected to touch the forelock or curtsy as well? She thrust her uncharitable thoughts aside as unworthy, even of somebody who had been snubbed as soundly as Callum had snubbed her. She should have known Shorelands was still an anachronism, a place where tradition ran too deep to be disturbed no matter what upheavals took place on the surface. Was that why Callum always seemed so mad with her—because she didn't call him *Mr* Callum, as the gardener's granddaughter should?

Gaby returned the welcoming kiss. Mrs Hoskins had always been kind to her. She was one of those plump but straight-backed women who, having reached fifty, never seemed to change. Gaby didn't expect similar thoughts to be running through Mrs Hoskins' mind, but she was standing back, her head on one side, her slightly bulbous blue eyes surveying Gaby minutely.

'My word, how old were you the last time you were here?' she asked. 'Eighteen, wasn't it? You haven't changed a bit.'

'Don't tell me that! I was flattering myself I'd improved.'

'You don't need to,' Mrs Hoskins told her firmly. 'You always were a taking little thing. Mr Justin was saying you'd altered tremendously, so I didn't quite know what to expect. A punk raver or something.'

Gaby laughed. 'If he'd been honest he'd have admitted I had to jog his memory before he remembered me at all. I was fourteen when he last saw me, but what are we standing here talking for? Come in and I'll make some tea.'

Mrs Hoskins began to walk with her to the kitchen, but she said, 'I can't stop, Gaby. I've so much to attend to at the manor. Mr Callum's met all the local bigwigs, of course, but this is the first time he's entertained formally. He's not particularly looking forward to it, but their hospitality has to be returned. The Armstrongs will be here, the Garretts from the Grange, the Pelhams from Granby Court, the vicar and some parish councillors. You know the sort of thing.'

'No, I don't,' Gaby contradicted. 'I never moved in those sort of circles.'

Mrs Hoskins smiled at her. 'No, I suppose not. You were too busy running through the woods like a wild thing or climbing trees or leaping dykes. I've never been able to imagine you settling to city life. Still working as an office temp?'

Like Callum, she didn't wait for confirmation or denial, but put her basket on the kitchen table and went on, 'I've brought you over some eggs, strawberries and salad stuffs. Don't you go buying anything like that because we've plenty up at the manor. I'll see you're kept supplied. It wouldn't be right, a Warren eating shop stuff when your grandfather grew fruit and veg for us all his life.'

'You're very kind,' Gaby replied, thankful she'd put away the groceries she'd bought that morning. Now she'd have to eat for two or, she amended as she saw the amount of produce coming out of the basket, a dozen. 'Are you sure you won't stop for tea?'

'When I've more time, then we'll have a good chat,' Mrs Hoskins promised. She turned towards the door, adding, 'My dear, whatever are you wearing wellingtons for on a lovely day like this?'

'To protect my legs while I'm clearing the garden,' Gaby replied, following her to the Mini. 'It's full of brambles, to say nothing of the creepy-crawlies in the long grass. I don't mind them when I can see them, but when they're crawling over my feet——'

'You shouldn't be doing hard work like that, a frail thing like you,' Mrs Hoskins interrupted. 'I'm sure Mr Callum would help by sending down——'

Gaby, not wanting to explain why she hadn't the least intention of being beholden to Callum, interrupted in her turn, 'I'm not as frail as I look, and I'm a Warren. Gardening comes naturally to me. Er—you seem to have adjusted to the changes at Shorelands well enough, so I gather you didn't mind the Hazletts leaving?'

'They never fitted. It was a bit of a shock, Mr Callum turning up out of the blue with nobody even suspecting his existence, but he's a gentleman, whatever anybody says,' Mrs Hoskins replied, her eyes kindling. 'It might not seem right to some, him in Mr Justin's proper place, but better Mr Callum than some new-fangled health farm. That never would have done for Shorelands, as everybody will see right enough when the dust's settled.'

She put her basket in the little car and climbed in ponderously after it. Gaby couldn't resist asking, 'The dust. . .you mean there's friction between the—the brothers?'

'You've been listening to local talk, and none of it comes from me,' Mrs Hoskins replied. 'All I'll say, Gaby, is that if you believe the half of what you hear you're believing too much. This is a small community and what people don't know they make up.'

'Of course,' Gaby replied, stepping back as Mrs Hoskins started the motor, telling herself she was a fool to expect the housekeeper to discuss her employer. Mrs Hoskins might have discussed the ins and outs of the situation with her grandfather, but they'd both been born and reared on the estate and she hadn't.

It seemed Callum had found himself one champion at least, and she couldn't expect any sympathy from Mrs Hoskins if she clashed with him again. Feeling very much an outsider, she went back into the kitchen and cheered herself up by eating the strawberries.

She ate so many that she didn't feel like working any longer. Weariness was overcoming her, and she supposed yesterday's long journey and an indifferent night's sleep were catching up on her. Yawning, Gaby wandered out to the shed, found Grandad's sorry-looking old deck-chair and set it up in a cleared section of the lawn under the shade of an old oak.

She took off her wellies and hat and flopped out, the sag in the chair suiting the way her body felt. She looked up, glimpsing the sky through a tracery of oak leaves. A sudden thought made her turn her head. The branch she used to climb out on to watch for Justin was still there.

Strange that she hadn't thought to check on that before. It had seemed so important in Paris. . . Her heavy eyelids closed, fluttered open and closed again.

She drifted off in a peaceful no man's land—no Harry, no Justin, no Callum—and slept as untroubled as a baby.

When she awoke she lay with her eyes closed for a while, lazily allowing the languor of an unaccustomed afternoon's nap to wear off. When she finally stirred it was to glance at her watch. Past seven o'clock. She'd slept for over three hours!

Gaby jerked into sitting position and groaned. She was stiff. She blamed the gardening, but obviously a deck-chair wasn't the best place to sleep for so long. She relaxed again, realising this was Shorelands, not Paris. There was no reason to feel guilty. She didn't have to rush around making up for lost time.

But something was wrong. It took Gaby a while to figure it out, but eventually she fell in. She was in the wrong place. She'd set up the deck-chair on the cropped area, and now she was in the long grass. Bewildered, she stared about her. The sun had moved round in the sky while she'd slept, and was shining on the cropped area. Somebody had lifted her, complete with deck-chair, further back under the tree into the shade.

And without disturbing her. Not the easiest task with an old and rickety chair. Who'd had the strength to carry it down the garden without awakening her?

Her mind, for some reason of its own, shot to Callum. She dismissed the idea. He was strong, but he wasn't gentle, and besides, he'd probably have enjoyed watching her burn. It must have been Justin, dropping by to apologise for the awkwardness over the dinner invitation.

A smile curved on her lips. Justin might be a shocking flirt, but his heart was obviously in the right place. How sweet of him to let her sleep on. Gaby tried to imagine him carefully bending over her, but the

picture wouldn't come together. All she could see was
Callum leaning towards her, his flinty eyes softening,
his strong arms reaching out. . .

'Oh, behave!' Gaby told herself crossly, getting up.
She walked gingerly through the long and then the
cropped grass, finally padding thankfully in her bare
feet on to the cool old flagstones of the kitchen.

She filled a long glass with orange juice, added a
couple of ice cubes and drank thirstily. What the devil
did she keep thinking about Callum for? Why did he
have to keep barging into what should have been a
straight conflict of purpose between the absent Harry
and the excitingly close Justin? She could only suppose
it was because Callum was like x, the unknown factor,
and unknown factors had always intrigued her.

Gaby knew she was oversimplifying, clutching at
straws, and she also knew why. It was because she still
couldn't sort out what was happening to her heart. If
only it would start whispering again, give her a clue.
Damn all men, Gaby thought, moodily fishing an ice
cube out of her empty glass and childishly licking it.
Then she damned herself for not really meaning it.

Because underlying her confusion was an excitement
headier than wine. She might not like what was happening to her, but she was fully, pulsatingly alive. She
felt as if she was waking from her dream world at last
and emerging into the real. It wasn't so safe, but the
excitement made her reckless, uncaring.

One thing was sure—she was too keyed up to face
the flatness of an evening alone in the gatehouse. She'd
have a bath and go to the Fisherman's Dream for that
promised chat with John, and see what else she could
find out about Callum and Justin.

Her purer self objected that she'd only be dishing
the dirt with the rest of the snoopers, but Gaby wasn't

feeling too pure just then. She was so impatient to be on her way that she jumped into the bath while the water was still running. She almost jumped out of her skin when somebody knocked on the bathroom door.

Gaby switched off the taps hurriedly. The gushing water must have masked the footsteps of whoever was out there. Her heart began to thump erratically as she realised that, not only had she forgotten to lock the back door, she hadn't bothered about the bathroom door, either. Freudian slips? she wondered. Did she really want somebody to walk in on her? Justin. . . Callum?

Her cheeks burned with guilty flame and she tried to sink her naked body under water that wasn't deep enough. She was frantically trying to froth up the sweet-smelling foam when the knocking came again and a voice asked, 'Are you in there, Gaby?'

Mrs Hoskins. Gaby felt giddy with relief, so light-headed that she responded laughingly, 'No, it's the nymph of the woods, the spirit of the river——'

'Do be serious, I'm in the most frightful pickle,' Mrs Hoskins all but wailed. 'Dinner is due to be served at eight and my waitress has let me down. It's Saturday night and I can't get a substitute anywhere at this short notice. Tom—you remember my husband Tom?— well, he can't manage twenty people all by himself and I'll be stuck in the kitchen. I'll die of shame if everything doesn't go off right. Will you come up and give a hand? Tom will tell you exactly what to do.'

Gaby's first reaction was of indignation. To wait at a table where she wasn't welcome as a guest? She'd rather die. 'I'm not a waitress,' she objected forthrightly. 'I'm not even a——'

She was about to say 'temp', but Mrs Hoskins broke

in urgently, 'At Shorelands it doesn't matter what we are, we all pull together in a crisis.'

That, Gaby thought, was a low blow. She swallowed her pride and grumbled, 'Oh, all right.'

'Bless you! Do you have a black dress?' Mrs Hoskins asked.

'Yes, but——'

'Good. You're so slender our standard uniforms would swamp you. What about black shoes and stockings?' Mrs Hoskins went on.

'I've got those, but——'

'Then there's no problem,' the housekeeper broke in again. 'I'll supply the cap and pinny. Oh, and there'll be ten pounds in it for you. A bit of extra money is always useful when you're on holiday, isn't it? Get up to the manor as soon as you can, my dear. The guests are having pre-dinner drinks in the great hall, but I want to keep to schedule.'

There was the sound of Mrs Hoskins' heavy feet walking away, the slam of the back door, and Gaby was left to have her quickest bath ever. She was still towelling herself dry as she ran up to her bedroom. She brushed her hair up into a pony-tail swiftly, having no time to tame damp tendrils that curled waywardly about her ears and neck.

What she'd been trying unsuccessfully to tell the housekeeper was that the sole black dress she'd brought with her wasn't the least bit suitable for a waitress. It was one of the dresses she'd packed in case Harry turned up to take her somewhere special. It was styled with true French chic, but teamed with a frilly pinny and cap she'd look like something out of a French bedroom farce. Very risqué.

Well, it was too late now, Gaby thought, wriggling into the seductive, figure-hugging black silk. The frock was long-sleeved and demure enough at the front, but the high neck was secured at the back with a pearl button, and there was a long, provocative slit until another pearl button secured it at the waist. The mid-calf skirt also had a long slit at the back to enable her to walk, or rather wiggle.

She had no practical black shoes, only the pair she'd bought to team with the dress, and they were nothing more than frivolous high heels secured to her dainty feet with slender straps. She couldn't imagine what Mrs Hoskins would think, but she didn't have time to worry about it. A hasty smidgen of dusky shadow on her eyelids, a touch of pink lipstick, a quick spray with light lily-of-the-valley perfume and she was ready.

The mirror showed her that she looked as she so often did if she wasn't careful—like sixteen playing twenty-two. That was usually her signal to start all over again, but she wasn't dating Harry tonight so it really didn't matter if she looked precocious rather than sophisticated. It would be miracle enough if she managed to totter around carrying trays without spilling soup in somebody's lap.

A snatched glance at her watch and Gaby fled down to her car. She zoomed around the curves of the tree-edged drive until the trees cleared and the road straightened like an arrow. Fraught as she was, her eyes softened as she approached the enduring flint and stone walls of the ancient farm-fortress.

The original building, the great hall in the centre, had later been flanked on either side by long, low, two-storeyed wings of the same flint and stone. Stretching back from them, and ranged around an enclosed cobbled courtyard were the dairy, smithy, stables, barns and other buildings necessary for complete medieval self-sufficiency.

Gaby absolutely adored the place, although she'd never penetrated further than the outbuildings and kitchen, where Mrs Hoskins had plied her with lemonade, scones and whatever else was going. She could have wept all over again for Justin's losing Shorelands, and she could almost understand why possessing it made Callum so feudal—almost, but not quite. There was something malicious at worst, callous at best about cutting out a legitimate brother just to puff up his own prestige.

Gaby felt a shiver of revulsion. At least, she thought it was that. Callum affected her nerves so powerfully that she was never too sure quite how she was reacting to him. She'd never been both attracted and repelled before. Like a moth to a flame, she thought, and shivered again.

She drove through the stone archway at the rear, bumped over the cobbles and parked next to the housekeeper's Mini, glad she at least knew her way to the kitchen. She was assailed by the most delicious smells as she walked in, and the first thing she felt was hunger. The second was pleasure at the welcoming smiles that lit Mrs Hoskins' and her husband's faces.

'Gaby, you angel, you have been prompt!' Mrs Hoskins exclaimed, but her smile faded as she took in Gaby's dress and shoes. 'Oh, dear, you look more like a guest than a waitress.'

'It's all I'd packed in black. A pinny will make it look more serviceable,' Gaby soothed, getting a kiss on the cheek from Tom Hoskins.

He was a tall man, as spare as his wife was plump, and he said, 'It's good to have you back, and, my word, your grandfather would be proud if he could see you now! We'll have a good talk later. As soon as you're kitted out, go to the dining-room, and don't you worry about a thing. I'll tell you what to do as we go along. I'll announce dinner now. It's just past eight and Mr Callum will be wondering what's going on.'

'Doesn't he know I'm helping out?' Gaby asked.

'He's been with his guests since seven, and we didn't know we were going to be let down until half-past,' Mrs Hoskins answered, giving Gaby her pinny and cap. 'There's a mirror over there by the door. Always check your appearance each time you go to the dining-room.'

Tom, in his sober black butler's suit, had already left, and Gaby went over to the long mirror. The pinny wasn't as substantial as she'd hoped. It had a bib top and was frilled all round. The cap was just as frilled, and she had trouble perching it on top of her ponytail. A chignon would have been better, she thought belatedly, jabbing in the securing pins the housekeeper handed her.

'Surely you haven't had to prepare the meal all by yourself?' Gaby asked, a pin still in her mouth.

'No, I had a couple of women from the village in but they both had to leave at seven-thirty to pick up their children from sitters. Neither could persuade them to do a couple of hours extra, it being Saturday night.' Mrs Hoskins noticed the slits in the back of Gaby's dress for the first time and exclaimed, 'Gaby! That dress isn't at all the sort of thing——'

'I know, but I'll treat all the guests like royalty, I won't turn my back on them,' Gaby reassured her, studying the effect of the pinny and cap from the front and deciding she didn't look at all the sort of thing from that view, either. 'Now, where's the dining-room?'

Mrs Hoskins brushed a distracted hand over her brow and opened the door on a long, narrow, flag-stoned passage with windows overlooking the court-yard. 'It's the last door along on the right. The one

facing you leads into the great hall, where Mr Callum's
entertaining his guests. It's a draughty place in winter,
but just right for weather like this. They'll be going
into the dining-room directly from the hall, so the door
you'll be using we call the service door.'

'Right, "once more unto the breach" and all that,'
Gaby breathed, and wiggled her way along the corridor. A babble of conversation greeted her as she
opened the door. She paused for a moment, blinking
at the beauty of the room. It was long and low, with an
oak-beamed ceiling and panelled walls. The oak table
gleamed with polish and silver, and had ample room
for the twenty people settling themselves around it.

Justin, heart-breakingly handsome in his dinner suit,
was at the foot of the table, and her eyes went
involuntarily to the top. There, seated in the great
carver as though he'd been born to it, was Callum. He
looked magnificently right, somehow. If Gaby hadn't
known Justin first, she'd have thought him the most
handsome man she'd ever seen, and even now she was
struck by a quality he had which Justin lacked. She
paused for a second, trying to define it. Power, she
thought, that was it. . .stemming, no doubt, from the
fact that he was rich.

It made it seem crazier than ever that he should need
Shorelands to satisfy some deep inner need. He certainly didn't give the impression of a man who had any
unfulfilled cravings, unless it was for Kate Armstrong,
a vision in flame-coloured chiffon at his right side. Very
bold with that red hair, Gaby thought with unaccustomed sourness, but it worked. Kate looked magnificent, too. How Justin must be suffering. . .

Nobody except Tom had noticed her. She moved
noiselessly over the thick-piled carpet towards the
massive sideboard where he was standing. He began

FREE GIFTS!

FREE BOOKS!

Play

CASINO JUBILEE

"Match'n Scratch" Game

PEEL OFF LABEL

PLACE LABEL INSIDE

**CLAIM UP TO
4 FREE BOOKS,
A FREE VICTORIAN
PICTURE FRAME AND A
SURPRISE GIFT!**

See inside ↗

NO RISK, NO OBLIGATION TO BUY... NOW OR EVER!

CASINO JUBILEE
"Match'n Scratch" Game

Here's how to play:

1. Peel off label from front cover. Place it in space provided at right. With a coin, carefully scratch off the silver box. This makes you eligible to receive one or more free books, and possibly other gifts, depending upon what is revealed beneath the scratch-off area.

2. You'll receive brand-new Harlequin Presents® novels. When you return this card, we'll rush you the books and gifts you qualify for ABSOLUTELY FREE!

3. If we don't hear from you, every month we'll send you 6 additional novels to read and enjoy. You can return them and owe nothing but if you decide to keep them, you'll pay only $2.47* per book, a saving of 28¢ each off the cover price. There is *no* extra charge for postage and handling. There are *no* hidden extras.

4. When you join the Harlequin Reader Service®, you'll get our subscribers-only newsletter, as well as additional free gifts from time to time just for being a subscriber!

5. You must be completely satisfied. You may cancel at any time simply by sending us a note or a shipping statement marked "cancel" or returning any shipment to us at our cost.

YOURS FREE!

This lovely Victorian pewter-finish miniature is perfect for displaying a treasured photograph and it's yours absolutely free — when you accept our no-risk offer!

*Terms and prices subject to change without notice. Sales tax applicable in NY.

CASINO JUBILEE
"Match'n Scratch" Game

CHECK CLAIM CHART BELOW FOR YOUR FREE GIFTS!

YES! I have placed my label from the front cover in the space provided above and scratched off the silver box. Please send me all the gifts for which I qualify. I understand I am under no obligation to purchase any books, as explained on the opposite page.

(U-H-P-09/91) 106 CIH ADEZ

Name

Address   Apt.

City   State   Zip

CASINO JUBILEE CLAIM CHART

🍒🍒🍒	WORTH 4 FREE BOOKS, FREE VICTORIAN PICTURE FRAME PLUS MYSTERY BONUS GIFT
🍒🔔🍒	WORTH 3 FREE BOOKS PLUS MYSTERY GIFT
🔔🔔🍒	WORTH 2 FREE BOOKS CLAIM N° 152B

HARLEQUIN "NO RISK" GUARANTEE

- You're not required to buy a single book — ever!
- You must be completely satisfied or you may cancel at any time simply by sending us a no or a shipping statement marked "cancel" or by returning any shipment to us at our cost. Either way, you will receive no more books; you'll have no obligation to buy.
- The free book(s) and gift(s) you claimed on the "Casino Jubilee" offer remains yours to ke no matter what you decide.

If offer card is missing, please write to: **Harlequin Reader Service** P.O. Box 1867, Buffalo, N.Y. 14269-186 lifting soup bowls and plates from a heated trolley on to a silver tray and filling them with soup from an ornate tureen.

'Serve each guest from the left side, and start with the lady on Mr Callum's right,' Tom whispered. 'Work your way down and around the table. Keep the crockery quiet.'

Gaby picked up the tray, wiggled towards the table and carefully served Kate. She felt the force of Cailum's frowning gaze on her and looked at him, wide-eyed. Her pulses raced as his expression changed. It reminded her forcibly of what had happened the last time she'd looked at him like that.

She was flustered. The silver tray trembled, the crockery rattled, and with a tremendous effort she recovered herself and moved on. When she returned to Tom he had another tray ready, and the serving continued without a hitch until she reached Justin.

'Gaby, you're a vision from my favourite fantasy,' he said appreciatively, not bothering to keep his voice low, his eyes glittering so wildly that she realised he'd been drinking more than the table wine. 'What do you think you're doing?'

'Trying not to spill soup into your lap,' she murmured repressively.

'I wish you would. It would give me an excuse to chase you back to the pantry.'

The tray trembled again and Gaby moved on, not risking a reply. Callum was watching; she knew it without having to look at him. She wondered what he was thinking, but it didn't do her nerves any good to dwell on that. When she made another trip to the sideboard for a fresh tray she quite forgot to keep her back to the guests, revealing the provocative slits in the back of her dress.

She cursed herself and hoped any watching guests didn't wonder what sort of an establishment Callum was running. When she finally served Callum, he said quietly, 'Thank you, Gaby.'

It had to be mere politeness, but she'd never known Callum be polite before. She looked at him in surprise, and if her expressive eyes were apprehensive it was because he had the infuriating and incomprehensible knack of making her nervous. She saw that slight frown again and, not knowing what else to do, she smiled.

The frown vanished. Callum smiled back and Gaby's world reeled.

CHAPTER SIX

GABY continued her work in a daze. Her heart was singing again, but it was to the wrong tune. Callum was nothing to her. All right, so he could draw a certain physical response from her. That had nothing to do with romance, and it was romantic dreams of Justin that had brought her back to Shorelands.

Sex. . .dreams. . .they had no solid worth. They were diversions, nothing more. If she needed any proof of that it was right here before her. Callum was talking most correctly—and most infuriatingly!—with Kate on his right or her mother on his left as though he'd never exchanged a toe-curling smile with the saucy little impromptu waitress.

And Justin was flirting with her with his eyes, as he flirted with all presentable women, and probably only to get back at Kate. Whatever struggle for supremecy he, Callum and Kate were locked into, Gaby told herself she wanted no part of it—and promptly suffered again all the anguish of being on the outside looking in.

When the soup dishes were cleared away and the main course served, Tom said to her, 'You nip along to the kitchen for your own meal. I'll press the service buzzer when I need you again. I had a good meal at six so I'm all right.'

Gaby left the dining-room, thankful for a break, and more than half inclined to blame her over emotional state on hunger. It was dim in the passage and she

searched in the last rosy glow of the setting sun for the
light switches and flicked them on.

She paused for a moment, looking out through one
of the leaded windows to the shadowed courtyard and
the only slightly brighter sky beyond. An old house
like this should be at peace, she thought, but it wasn't
and neither was she. Gaby sighed and walked on to the
kitchen where the bright homeliness lightened her
mood.

Mrs Hoskins, stacking dishes into one of the dish
washers, looked round with a smile. 'Well, the worst is
over and we've survived. The desserts are cold and
they're all ready. I suppose Tom has sent you back for
your meal?'

'If it's not too much trouble,' Gaby replied, sitting
down at the table and thankfully easing off her high
heels. 'I've come to the conclusion that the lot of a
waitress isn't a happy one.'

The housekeeper chuckled as she put a plate of
succulent roast beef in front of Gaby and flanked it
with a dish of vegetables and a gravy bowl. 'Put
yourself on the outside of that and you'll feel a lot
better. You're so skinny, I don't suppose you eat
enough to keep a sparrow alive.'

'Skinny is when the bones show in all the wrong
places, and mine don't. I eat very well,' Gaby told her,
and then set about her meal in a ravenous way that
proved it.

'I know you girls. All your money goes on clothes
instead of food,' Mrs Hoskins retorted. She put a
coffee-tray on the table and sat down herself. 'A
breather won't do me any harm, either. Milk and
sugar, Gaby?'

'Yes, please.' Gaby carried on eating, but when the
housekeeper was comfortably sipping her coffee, she

added, 'Sam Gibson told me yesterday that Mrs Foley, who used to clean the gatehouse for me, is living here now. How come she couldn't help out tonight?'

'She's on a fortnight's holiday with her children, staying over the border in Norfolk with her mother.' Mrs Hoskins was silent for a while, then continued, 'So you've been talking to Sam. If that means you're selling the gatehouse, why don't you deal with Mr Callum direct? I'm sure he'll make you a good offer. He doesn't like strangers inside his gates.'

'I know that,' Gaby retorted. 'What's he guarding here, the crown jewels?'

'Mostly I think it's us. He's not always here himself to see we're all right, and such dreadful things do happen these days,' Mrs Hoskins answered, oblivious to Gaby's ire.

Gaby promptly felt ashamed of herself. 'I suppose so, but I haven't put the gatehouse on the market yet. I want to get it sorted out first. I suppose I'll have to sell, but it will be a wrench.'

'Yes, well, you're a Warren. Shorelands is in your blood, just as it's in Mr Callum's, although neither of you grew up here.'

'Is that what you really think?' Gaby asked. 'You don't believe Mr Durand——' not for anything was she going to say 'Mr Callum' '—is just amusing himself playing squire and putting Justin's nose out of joint?'

'Mr Justin's old enough to look after his own nose, and I've warned you about listening to nasty people who don't know anything,' the housekeeper replied pithily.

'Yes, but if Shorelands is in anybody's blood, it must be strongest of all in Justin's!' Gaby exclaimed.

'Sometimes the blood thins.'

Gaby put down her knife and fork and stared at the

housekeeper. 'You've switched loyalties, you of all people. . .'

'I haven't switched anything,' Mrs Hoskins denied hotly. 'I've always had a soft spot for Mr Justin and I always will. Show me the woman who hasn't, no matter what her age. He's got a way with him, there's no denying that, but I'm for whatever's best for Shorelands, and that's Mr Callum. He's dependable.'

'Is he, indeed?' Gaby breathed. 'Well, good old *Mr* Callum. He's got it made, hasn't he? Let's not bother ourselves about Justin, who's never had a chance to prove himself, and through no fault of his own!'

The service buzzer sounded. Gaby suddenly felt limp. 'End of round one,' she said with a shaky laugh. She quickly finished her coffee and reached for her shoes.

'So it's Mr Justin with you, is it?' Mrs Hoskins said grimly. 'You watch yourself, my girl, or you'll come an almighty cropper.'

'I'm not Alice in Wonderland, and I'm not a waitress either, so don't think you can lecture me,' Gaby retorted hotly. 'I'm wearing a cap and pinny as a favour, not because I have to.'

She didn't know where her sudden flash of temper came from, but to her surprise Mrs Hoskins smiled. 'You're old Warren's granddaughter all right. He never had any patience with people who stepped out of place, my word he didn't. Now be off with you, and fight those who need fighting, not me.'

Gaby smiled ruefully and fled. She and Tom were kept very busy, clearing the main course, serving the dessert, then the cheeses and biscuits and coffee. The ridiculously high heels she was wearing weren't meant for so much standing, and the gardening ache in her back began to play her up. When she could she stretched her back to ease it and lifted each aching foot in turn for a brief respite.

More than once she caught Callum's eyes on her, and promptly tried to look as though this waitressing stint hadn't turned into one long endurance test. It was Justin's eyes she was avoiding now. He had been drinking too much and he was doing everything but blow kisses at her.

Probably it was only to make Kate jealous, but he was drawing unwelcome attention to her. Other guests were throwing her curious glances. Gaby wondered if they thought she'd dressed in such spectacular fashion just to attract him, and she was embarrassed. More than that there was a depressing and growing knot of sadness within her.

She'd returned to Shorelands to break the hold her dreams of Justin had over her but she'd never expected to have to endure the pain of seeing them tarnish and dim. A quick, clean, antiseptic break by selling the gatehouse was what she'd had in mind. But she'd met her hero again as an adult, not an uncritical girl, and found him flawed. It hurt dreadfully. She'd never suspected letting go of a dream could be so painful.

Gaby felt strangely guilty, too. Almost tarnished herself. She'd accused Mrs Hoskins of switching loyalties and she didn't want to do the same thing herself. Not now, when Justin was losing out all round to Callum. It was one thing to lose a hero, another to kick him when he was down. So Justin had had a few drinks too many and was making a fool of himself and of her—so what? He had good reason for wanting to forget his troubles, and she wasn't exactly a full-time saint herself.

So Gaby reasoned, but still her dreams crumbled and still her sadness grew. Harry, she thought, I have to get back to Harry. If it's perfection I want, he's the closest I can get to it.

Her eyes went involuntarily to Callum. No, he wasn't perfect. He grabbed what he wanted regardless of who got hurt. Suddenly Gaby's fantasies, adrift from Justin, speculated what it would be like to be wanted by Callum. Her nerves tingled and her skin contracted, making her come out in goose-pimples all over.

She knew what it was like to be wanted by Callum. It was something she'd been trying very hard to forget. She knew what it felt like to be crushed into his arms and not to care, to be burned by his kisses until she flamed for more. It was more than she knew about Justin or Harry, and she had the frightening feeling that Callum had already stamped her as his own.

'One more round with the coffee-tray and I think that will be it,' Tom said to her.

Gaby stared at him blankly.

'Are you all right?' he asked anxiously. 'If it's all been too much for you, I can cope now.'

'No, no, I'm fine, thanks. My mind was wandering, that's all.' Gaby saw Tom was still regarding her strangely. She forced a smile and said in self-mockery, 'You know how it is when you're having fun.'

She picked up the coffee-tray and began the round again. Most refused, but when she reached Justin he just lolled back in his chair and grinned foolishly at her. Gaby didn't wait for him to say anything, but began filling his cup regardless. She was halfway through when Justin stroked her thigh. The pot in her hand jerked and coffee spilled in the saucer.

'My god, suspenders and stockings,' he said thickly. 'Not those damned awful tights, but suspenders.'

There was an awful hush. Gaby's cheeks burned. Before she could move away Justin's unsteady fingers groped through the black silk, clutched her suspender and pinged it.

'Justin!' Callum's voice from the top of the table was harsh.

'Don't worry, bruv.' Justin laughed and his arm encircled Gaby's waist, pulling her against him. She hurriedly lifted the silver tray up out of danger, unconsciously tautening the black silk of her dress and outlining her firm young breasts. 'Gaby doesn't mind at all. What d'you think she's all tricked up like this for? She always did fancy me. Used to hide away to watch me. . .thought I didn't see her, but I did.' Justin's arm squeezed tighter and he looked up at her. 'Tell him, Gaby. Tell 'em all how it was. You were too young then, but you're not now, are you, love?' He lowered his head and nuzzled her bosom.

Gaby, dying of shame, tried unavailingly to free herself. Suddenly Justin's arm was wrenched away from her, Callum's strong hands were on her waist and she was lifted clear.

'Come on, old man, I'll get you up to bed,' Callum was saying to Justin. 'You've had one over the eight.'

'Get your hands off me, you watered-down bastard of a Durand,' Justin objected, his slurred voice gaining invective strength with each word. 'We true Durands can hold our liquor. We true Durands——'

Gaby waited to hear no more. She stalked out of the room, along the passage, stripping off her cap and apron as she went. In the kitchen she slammed them down on the table. Mrs Hoskins wasn't there, so Gaby stormed on, out into the courtyard, into her car, and drove out of the darkened archway a lot faster than she had come in.

She was shaking when she reached the gatehouse.

How could Justin have humiliated her like that? Exposing her adolsecent yearnings, mocking them, making her feel she'd been stripped naked before Callum and everybody who was anybody in the neighbourhood. Now they'd all believe, as Justin did, that she'd dressed provocatively to lead him on. Just another silly girl throwing herself at his feet.

Gaby's cheeks burned anew as she realised she hadn't been so very far from doing that—but that was before she'd discovered the real man didn't measure up to her romantic hero, before she'd met Callum.

Before she'd met Callum! That was the crux of the matter. He was the one who made her so self-conscious. If he hadn't been there she'd have coped a whole lot better instead of blushing and dying on her feet. Grief, this place was such a hotbed of gossip that she could just imagine the rumours that would be circulating tomorrow! 'Do you remember old Warren's granddaughter? Well, there she was, all tarted up like a stage waitress in a naughty revue to catch Justin's eye and. . .'

Gaby closed her eyes in horror. She didn't need to be told the gossip would grow with the telling and the sympathy wouldn't be on her side. She was the outsider. People would say it served her right because you couldn't entice a man like Justin without expecting some action. There'd be winks and sniggers and everybody would be watching to see what happened next.

Her first instinct was to throw herself into bed, pull the covers over her head and stay there, but she was much too keyed up to sleep. The prospect of hours of tossing and turning didn't exactly grab her. She had to calm down first, get everything into perspective.

She was still shaking. She tried to laugh at herself. She'd been groped, not raped, and the only harm done was that it had happened in public. Sighing, she pulled the ribbon from her pony-tail, shook her hair down and put Grandad's old coffee percolator on to heat. She walked around the room while she waited, too nervy to sit down for more than a couple of seconds at a time.

The night was so quiet, so still, that she heard the car from a long way away. It was powerful and moving fast. It took her a few more seconds to realise it was coming this way. She was puzzled. If any of the guests had left early, they'd be using the main gate. Nobody had any reason to come this way. Unless. . .unless it was Justin with that fixed idea in his head that she was his for the taking.

She flew to the door. It was already locked, but she had to struggle with the bolt, stiff because it was never used, before she could slam it home. There—even with drunken strength, he'd never get through that. The car stopped, there was the slam of the door and footsteps on the flagged pathway.

This was the only lit room, so he'd come here. Gaby waited, heart beating unevenly, and nibbling her beautifully manicured thumbnail without actually biting it. He'd managed to get the car here without wrapping it round a tree, so he couldn't be too bad. Perhaps the night air had sobered him a bit, perhaps she'd be able to reason with him, perhaps. . .

The footsteps stopped, knuckles rapped against the old wood of the door, and, although Gaby had been expecting it, she jumped. 'Go away,' she said. 'Sleep it off in the car. I'm not letting you in here.'

'Gaby.' The voice was deep, calm and sober. 'It's Callum.'

'Oh.' She fumbled with the bolt again, got the door unlocked and stepped back.

Callum came in, big, immaculate in his dinner suit and white shirt, making her nerves jump for an entirely different reason. 'I came to apologise for Justin,' he said.

He was overpoweringly close and she moved away, pushing her hair distractedly back from her face. 'It wasn't your fault.'

'He'd been drinking all day. I should have foreseen some sort of incident. Are you all right?'

Callum was looking at her so searchingly that she felt she had to reassure him, though heaven knew why. She parted her lips in what she hoped was a smile, and replied as perkily as she could, 'I've had jollier evenings, but I'm all right now, thanks.'

There was an awkward silence. Gaby was embarrassed. The constraint between them seemed worse, somehow, than the awful scene with Justin. The percolator began to bubble, incredibly noisy in the silent room. They both looked at it. 'Am I invited?' Callum asked.

'Surely you have to get back to your guests? I'm very grateful for your coming here, but——'

'A few minutes this way or that won't make much difference,' he cut in brusquely. 'On the other hand, if I'm not welcome I can always go.'

For some reason tears smarted Gaby's eyes. Hurriedly she turned her back on him, opening a wall cabinet to reach for cups. 'It's a f-full pot,' she said offhandedly, hoping her slight stammer hadn't revealed how overwrought she was. The cups rattled when she set them out, and rattled again as she put the spoons in the saucers. She just couldn't control her shaking hands.

This kitchen's too small for the two of us, she thought. He's shrinking it, taking up all the available space, making it difficult for me to breathe. She knew, though, that the problem was an emotional and not a physical one. She was just so dreadfully, dreadfully conscious of him.

'Black or white?' she asked.

'Black, one sugar.'

Gaby spilled the sugar. 'You're not all right, you're a nervous wreck,' Callum said, coming close behind her and brushing back her hair to see her face.

His fingers touched her neck, accidentally she was sure, but still her vulnerable flesh quivered and ached for more. And the secret whisper in her heart started up again, murmuring things she could scarcely believe. How could it, after being infuriatingly constant for so long, suddenly become just as infuriatingly capricious?

Gaby managed to pour the coffee so it actually went into the cups, cleared her throat and replied feverishly, 'That's waitressing for you! A total mind-blower when you've never done it before. I'd no idea what a strain it would be, trying not to drop a tray or spill things over people.'

'You're babbling, stop it,' Callum ordered, putting his hands on her shoulders and turning her to face him.

She was so close to him. Another inch and she could rest her head against his chest, close her eyes and forget the embarrassing scene with Justin had ever happened. Callum could make her forget, she was sure of that. She felt herself swaying towards him, weak with a mixture of exhaustion and longing. One of his hands moved from her shoulder to her back, gently pulling her towards him, then his fingers slipped through the slit in the black silk and touched her bare back.

A shock passed through her entire nervous system, her flesh felt seared and she gave an involuntary gasp.

She felt Callum tauten and then he thrust her away from him. 'You were right,' he said roughly, 'I should be getting back to my guests.'

Gaby's emotions couldn't adjust quickly enough. She only knew she didn't want him to go away, and she faltered, 'But your coffee. . .'

'I'll skip it, thanks.' Then he was gone, closing the door with unnecessary force behind him.

Gaby felt rejected, and, of all the emotions she'd experienced since returning to Shorelands, that was by far the worst.

What sleep she had that night came in fitful patches interspersed with long periods of wide-eyed wakefulness. She watched dawn lighten the room from inky blackness to silvery grey, feeling too comatose to do anything but feel sorry for herself. Inevitably, reaction set in and she sprang out of bed. If she hadn't managed to sleep away her depression, she could certainly walk it off. Shorelands was the place for that.

A few minutes later, kitted out in shorts, sweater and sturdy sandals, she stepped out of the cottage into a strange fairy-tale world. A mist lay a foot or two above the ground, and out of it the trees rose like silent, disembodied monsters. All it needed was an owl to hoot, but Gaby wasn't timid. She loved the eerie beauty of mornings like this at Shorelands, and the only reason she hesitated was to make up her mind which way to walk.

A sudden raucous squabble among gulls tempted her towards the sea, but then the plaintive call of a curlew had her skirting the trees and heading for the marshes. It was a long walk, but that was what she needed, and if she sat quietly at her favourite spot on the reeded banks of the dyke she could count how many species of wild duck she could spot.

She knew every inch of Shorelands, and she set out sure-footedly along paths the uninitiated would never know were there. The sun was rising like a great blurred orange ball, its heat not yet sufficient to steam away the low-lying mist. Gaby was beginning to feel happy again. This place she loved was beginning to work its magic over her again. It was only the people who lived here who mucked it up, and she intended to stay well clear of them today.

When she reached the bank of the dyke she crept quietly along the path at the base of it so as not to disturb the wild birds. Only when she reached her favourite place did she climb cautiously towards the top.

'Shh!'

Gaby was too startled to even scream. A hand reached up and pulled her down. She found herself lying full length on the damp grass beside the lean, hard body of Callum Durand. He was wearing shorts, too, and as their bare legs touched his arm came around her shoulders, pinning her down.

Her heart began to beat so loudly that she felt sure he could hear it, but he just put his lips close to her ear and whispered, 'Herons.'

'And the same to you,' she murmured, her sense of fun getting the better of her. He grinned, and suddenly she knew there was no place on earth she would rather be than lying on a damp bank beneath a ghostly layer of mist with Callum's arm around her. His dark hair was clinging damply to his forehead, and she supposed hers was doing the same, but all she was aware of was that, for the moment, they were like fellow conspirators as they looked down into the dyke.

The water level was low, so the hot dry weather must have lasted for some time, and walking in it with quaint daintiness for their size was a pair of herons, dipping their bills every so often in search of food. 'It's good to see a sight like that outside a bird sanctuary,' Callum said softly.

He was looking at her again, and her senses tingled as she felt his breath on her ear. She dared not look at him, afraid her eyes would reveal what she was feeling. She was almost afraid to speak as well. They had never yet managed to be alone together without antagonism flaring between them, and she didn't want to mar these magic moments.

'It's good to see the marsh is still here,' she replied eventually.

'What made you say that?'

There was a snap in Callum's voice, and surprise turned Gaby's face to his. She thought she'd found a safe subject, but it seemed she hadn't. 'Because so much marshland has already been drained and filled in to grow crops. My grandfather was very bitter about it. He called it driving out the wildlife for a few more bushels of wheat. He dreaded it happening at Shorelands after the Durands left—the other Durands, I mean,' she added awkwardly. 'He said it wasn't necessary, anyway, because the reeds are a paying crop when they're cut for thatch after Christmas.'

'I see,' Callum said.

But it was Gaby who was wary now. She was remembering what Sam Gibson had said about Callum 'fussing over the marshes', and asked uneasily, 'You're not going to fill them in, are you?'

'No.'

'Then why did you snap my head off?' She was distracted by a sudden movement and turned her head away. A curlew had swooped down to join the herons, spearing its curved beak into the mud in its own hunt for food. Something gently brushed her hair. Callum's lips? She wasn't sure, and yet her spine contracted deliciously.

'I wondered how much you knew,' he said.

'About what?' Gaby was totally bewildered now. He seemed almost to be playing a game with her. She wished she knew the rules—or even if there were any. With Callum, she doubted it.

'It doesn't matter. I just wanted to be certain whose side you're on.'

Gaby, against her better judgement, looked at him again. He must have been out at dawn as she had, but he'd shaved first. His jaw was smooth. She rather thought he'd used aftershave, too, but she couldn't be sure. It was subtle, beguiling, and she'd have to lean closer. . . She found herself doing just that and checked herself.

Dear heaven, what was happening to her? She was losing herself in irrelevancies, letting Callum's physical presence overwhelm her. She had to think frantically to remember what they were talking about, and, when she did, she objected, 'I'm not on anybody's side.'

'Yes, you are.' Callum seemed amused. 'Like it or not, you're on my side. You just can't help yourself.'

Words failed her. Her eyes widened in disbelief and she blinked at his incredible arrogance.

'Little owl,' Callum murmured, shaking his head. 'You never learn, do you?'

The next thing Gaby knew she was on her back and he was leaning over her. He caught her lips parted in surprise, and kissed them lightly, teasingly, as though teaching her a lesson. Against her will, against every instinct, Gaby trembled and melted. There didn't seem to be any part of her his lips hadn't touched and weakened.

Callum raised his head and frowned, quite why she didn't know, but when his mouth covered hers again he wasn't teasing at all.

CHAPTER SEVEN

GABY'S eyes closed and the world with its herons and mists and ghostly images drifted away. There was only Callum now, and the delicious sensations he was arousing in her. His lips were searching, but not cruel and aggressive as they'd been before. Loving, that was what they were, and she surrendered herself to love.

The secret whisper in her heart was satisifed at last. She was thrilled and yet at peace. She'd finally matched the purity of feeling Justin had once inspired in her. Her heart hadn't, as she'd supposed, been constant to Justin—but to an ideal. She'd been saved for this and she was grateful. She was so truly grateful.

Callum murmured huskily against her lips, 'You're not Justin's. You're mine.'

The satisfaction in his voice brought Gaby back to reality with a jolt. She opened her eyes and gasped with a pain that had no physical cause. Callum's eyes were alight not with love but triumph.

And then she understood. Callum had taken Shorelands and Kate from Justin. She was next on his hit list because he believed Justin wanted her as well—and she'd very nearly fallen into the trap. Revolted, Gaby put her hands against his chest and tried to thrust him away. 'What's this, squire?' she asked bitterly. 'Open season on the gardener's granddaughter?'

Callum released her at once, a flash of anger in his eyes. 'If you're going to start on that damned squire nonsense again——'

'Oh, stop being such a hypocrite,' she broke in

crossly. 'You get your kicks from being Squire Durand. You're sick! You slam Justin for grabbing me in public, but never waste the chance to behave the same yourself in private. At least Justin's honest. You're just——'

Words failed her and she jumped to her feet. Startled, the herons rose in noisy and cumbersome flight, creating panic among the wildfowl in the marsh beyond the dyke. For chaotic moments the air was full of squawks and cries as snipe, mallard and curlews flapped or paddled away. When it was quiet again, Callum said dangerously, 'Yes, Gaby, what am I?'

'You're wasting your time.' Gaby's hurt and anger were draining away, leaving her feeling lost and dejected. 'I'm not playing any of your games.'

'What if I told you I'm not playing games?' he asked.

'I wouldn't believe you.'

Callum looked down at her with an intentness that made her feel even more uncomfortable. Then he tilted her face up to his and smiled in a way that made her breathless. 'Reserve judgement, Gaby,' he said softly. 'Will you do that much for me?'

She wondered wildly whyever she'd thought Justin had all the charm. Callum, damn him, had very neatly taken all the wind out of her sails and she could only bluster, 'Why should I?'

'Because I'm asking you to, and because I'm also declaring the season on the gardener's granddaughter closed. You and I started off on the wrong foot and we've been out of step ever since. It's all my fault, so I'm stepping back into line. Good enough?'

All sorts of objections rose to Gaby's lips, but somehow they refused to be spoken, and he didn't wait longer than a second or two before taking her consent for granted. His arm came around her shoulders and she stiffened. 'Relax,' he told her as he led her down to the path, 'I'm just being friendly. I don't want to lose you in the mist.'

Gaby found herself walking with him, but she protested, 'There's not much mist left.'

Callum chose to ignore that, and asked, 'What brought you out in it in the first place?'

'I love cobweb mornings.' She felt his glance and explained, 'It's what my grandfather used to call them.'

'I wish I'd met him. Do you miss him very much?'

'No. I think Shorelands and the Durands were more important to him than his own family,' she said.

'Did you resent that?'

'No. He accepted me the way I was and I accepted him the way he was. We got on fine, but we were never what you'd call close,' Gaby explained.

'Then you're not hanging on to the gatehouse because it was his?'

'No. I was only at Shorelands for my summer holidays between the ages of fourteen and eighteen, but I fell in love with it, too.' Gaby didn't know why she was telling him all this, but she felt compelled to justify herself. 'I suppose. . .because I'm a Warren. My famly has lived here almost as long as yours. It must be something in the genes.'

Callum didn't say anything and she thought it was time he did, so she asked, 'Why *did* you buy Shorelands?'

'I fell in love with it myself. I'm not very sensible when I'm in love. Are you?'

The question caught her unawares. She cast a fleeting look at him, saw that intentness in his eyes again and hurriedly looked away. Why, oh, why did she let him keep turning the tables on her? Her heart was thumping erratically again and she could only mumble, 'I don't suppose anybody is.'

'Is it because of your *man* friend that you're con
sidering selling?'

Harry! Good heavens, whatever was she going to do
about Harry? Her mind, though, refused to concen
trate on the problem, and she could only think how
much she hated the way Callum always emphasised
man when he referred to Harry. 'Yes,' she replied, not
knowing what else to say. 'Keeping the gatehouse
simply isn't practical.'

'And are you going to be practical? Or is he the
practical one?' he pressed.

'It's my gatehouse and my decision,' Gaby replied
positively. 'If I sell, it will be because I don't need—
mean want—it any longer.'

She expected him to pressurise her further, make
her an offer that would sway her against his will. She
couldn't think of any reason other than the gatehouse
to account for his abrupt change of manner to her
Callum, though, remained unpredictable. He merely
said, 'Fair enough,' and dropped the subject.

Not knowing whether to feel relieved or frustrated,
she looked around her and exclaimed, 'This isn't the
way to the gatehouse!'

'No, the manor's closer. I'm sure you're as hungry as
I am, and having breakfast together seems as good a
way as any of celebrating our new relationship.'

It sounded very intimate to Gaby. On the other
hand, his arm around her shoulders was strictly com
panionable. Perhaps she could trust him. Perhaps she
really didn't care if she couldn't. Oh, hell, she thought,
how did I get myself into this fix?

More to make conversation than anything, she put a
hand up to the collar of her jumper, pulled it away
from her neck and said, 'It's getting hot.'

'Take your jumper off,' Callum suggested.

'I can't. I haven't got anything on underneath.'

'I know,' he said.

Gaby blushed, shot him an indignant look and saw he was smiling down at her. It was a smile that invited her to smile back, and after a moment's hesitation she did. They walked on and she began to feel pleasantly light-hearted. Callum was beginning to make her aware of how grim and earnest her life had become, how serious and cautious her relationship with Harry was. It was almost as if a burden she hadn't known she'd accumulated was falling from her shoulders.

Callum, it seemed, could be fun—and how long was it since she'd had any fun? She was thinking that one through when he asked, 'Can you cook?'

'Sort of,' she replied, her mind still exploring the possibilities of a relationship based on nothing heavier than mutual enjoyment.

'So can I, sort of. We should be able to rustle up something between us. It's Mrs Hoskins' day off, and Mrs Foley, her Sunday substitute, is on holiday.'

Gaby stopped short and exclaimed indignantly, 'So that's how it is! I'm not good enough to invite for dinner, but all right for breakfast providing I cook it myself. You've got a nerve!'

'Did it hurt so much not being invited to dinner?' Callum asked, stooping to kiss her on the nose. 'I'm sorry. I wouldn't hurt you for the world, but the arrangements were all made and one more would have made the numbers uneven.'

Among the many things Gaby objected to was being kissed on the nose like that. It seemed so much more personal and loving somehow than when he was trying to draw her soul through her lips, and damn near succeeding! 'I'm not hurt, I'm angry,' she exploded. 'I don't like being patronised or treated like a bimbo.

Nor do I appreciate being lied to. You're not the so
of man to worry about piffling things like uneve
numbers. I'll cook my own breakfast in my own hom
thanks!'

She swung away from him, but Callum caught her b
the arm and pulled her back. 'If I lied it was to save m
own face, not to get at you,' he told her quietly. 'Th
truth is, I couldn't endure an evening of Justin droolin
all over you. He's no good for you, Gaby.'

'I see, and you think I haven't the sense to work tha
out for myself?'

'No,' he corrected, 'I was the one not being to
sensible at the time.'

Gaby's legs felt weak, but not with fury. She bega
to walk on for fear they would collapse under he
altogether. She was remembering Callum saying, 'I'
not very sensible when I'm in love.' That couldn't hav
been what he meant, though. They hadn't known eac
other for forty-eight hours yet!

Gaby thought bleakly that a stop-watch couldn't b
held on falling in love, but then, she was vulnerable
and a man less vulnerable than Callum she couldn
imagine. And there was Kate. She would be mad t
forget about Kate. No, whatever true feeling there wa
must be all on her side. The most—or the worst—sh
could expect of Callum was that he was trying t
romance the gatehouse away from her.

She was muddled, though, and not too sure abou
anything. Perhaps he sensed her indecision, because h
raised her right hand, looked at the healing blotch o
her palm where he'd dug out the thorn, then kissed i
'Nearly better,' he said. 'Are we nearly friends agai
Gaby?'

She didn't answer because she didn't really kno

what to say, so he pressed, 'What if I cook and you supervise? Will that get me out of the doghouse?'

Gaby bit her full lower lip and grumbled, 'I think you make your own doghouse and run in and out of it as you please.'

'Woof, woof,' he barked.

Gaby laughed. She shouldn't have, but she really couldn't help herself. In the end, they shared cooking breakfast. They got in each other's way, but now they'd learned how to laugh together they didn't stop laughing. Callum grilled two steaks, while she poached the eggs he insisted on having on top. She also made the toast and tea and served up.

The kitchen, stone-walled and stone-floored, was cool, but windows on two sides ensured it was also sunny. When they were seated at the scrubbed pine table Gaby looked at her meal in despair. It was far too much. Decisively she halved her steak and lifted it, complete with one of her poached eggs on top, and put it on Callum's plate. 'The rest I can manage,' she explained. 'There's no sense in spoiling my appetite before I start.'

Callum looked at her in that disconcertingly intent way of his, made up his mind that she meant what she said, and smiled. 'You must come to breakfast more often.'

Gaby was glowing. Not from the warmth of cooking or the harassment of poaching eggs properly for once in her life, but from happiness. It was like a bubble inside her, expanding by the minute, making her feel deliciously irresponsible. She said wickedly, 'So long as I don't mind sitting at the kitchen table? Well, I don't, but I'm surprised the squire——'

It was as far as she got. Callum picked up his plate

and hers, and strode out of the kitchen with them. She'd overestimated their new-found rapport.

'Callum!' she exclaimed, grabbing her knife and fork and the tea-tray and following him. 'Callum, I was only——' She was talking to thin air. She caught up with him in the dining-room, which looked bare with the silverware put away, and empty with just the two of them.

'This suit you better?' Callum asked, putting her meal down in the place Kate had occupied the night before.

'No, it doesn't. It's much too formal for breakfast,' she replied crossly.

He picked up the plates again and walked out. Gaby followed him with the tea-tray, exasperated. She thought they were returning to the kitchen, but he turned off into a small room with a reasonably sized table set in front of a pair of latticed windows.

'The breakfast parlour,' he said, putting the plates down, taking the tray from her, and putting it down too. He held out a chair for her and, when she was seated, sat down himself and began to eat. Gaby followed suit, but she grumbled, 'There was no need for "follow my leader". I was only teasing.'

He didn't react. The rift was opening between them again and she didn't want it to get any wider. 'What,' she suggested tentatively, 'if I stopped making cracks about your being the squire?'

'It might give us time to eat our breakfast while it's still hot. It's Shorelands I went for, not some outmoded title.'

'Oh!' If Gaby sounded dubious, it wasn't because she doubted Callum, but because she couldn't understand why Justin and Sam were convinced he got a kick out of lording it over the locals.

Callum couldn't have liked the sound of her 'Oh!'. He sounded grim as he asked, 'I suppose now you're thinking I only bought Shorelands to put Justin's nose out of joint?'

She was terribly tempted to ask 'Did you?', because she did so want to know, but there was already a frown between Callum's dark eyebrows so she resisted the impulse. Instead she said lightly, 'Me, I'm not thinking anything. I'm reserving judgement, remember?'

The frown vanished. Callum's big hand came over and ruffled her hair with an affection that tugged at her heart. 'You really are a darling,' he murmured.

Gaby's heart pounded. Confused, she looked down at her plate.

'A blushing darling,' Callum teased.

Her spirit rebelled. After complaining about being treated like a bimbo, here she was acting like one. 'Make the most of it,' she advised. 'It doesn't happen often.'

'Don't tell me that. You look absolutely adorable.'

Gaby stopped defending and came out on the attack. 'Stop flirting with me.'

'You might just as well tell me to stop breathing. You're lovely.'

'No, I'm not,' she contradicted. 'Nothing about me is quite right.'

'From where I'm sitting everything looks absolutely perfect.'

Gaby wished she could believe him, but she was too honest, and she'd never been able to face herself in the mirror without also facing up to obvious imperfections. She thought she knew how to check him, and said bluntly, 'You're beginning to sound like Justin.'

Callum didn't lose his cool. He just told her, 'If ever you're confused, I'm the brother who is sincere.'

She knew then that she couldn't keep this up. He was trumping her on every trick. She slanted the conversation another way by asking, 'Where is Justin?'

'Sleeping it off. He'll be mad when he knows what he's missed.' Callum saw her eyebrows rise and explained. 'A girl with fathomless eyes walking like a dream out of a cobweb morning——'

Gaby interrupted, 'Callum, don't.'

'I know. You don't want me to flirt with you. Is Justin the barrier?'

'No.' Gaby felt they were skating on thin ice, and she was so afraid of falling through that she added in self-mockery, 'He belongs to a lost time when the world was young and beautiful.'

'You poor old lady!' Callum saw a responsive smile quiver on her lips, and pursued, 'If it's not Justin, it must be your *man* friend. What's his name?'

They'd both finished eating and Gaby poured the tea. 'Harry Preston.'

'What's he like?'

'Just about perfect,' Gaby said, giving him his cup.

Callum stirred his tea, but his eyes remained on her. 'Are my faults so very bad, Gaby?'

There was a caressing note in his voice, and her heart began to beat to a wild and wayward rhythm. He's still playing with me, she thought, and I'm losing. I'm losing out all round. She sipped her tea as if considering before she answered, 'I don't really know you.'

'I'm doing my best.'

'Yes, but it really isn't necessary,' she retorted with a touch of asperity. 'If I sell the gatehouse it will obviously be to you. I can't think of anybody else who could outbid you.'

'Are you really so hard up you have to sell?' Callum asked.

'No, I'm not.'

'Then why are you working like a Trojan on that jungle of a garden, waiting on tables for a few measly pounds——'

Gaby put down her tea cup with a thump. 'I'm a Warren, I like gardening. It must be something else that's in the genes. As for waitressing last night, I was doing a favour for Mrs Hoskins, that's all. The trouble with you, Callum, is that you've heard little bits about me from Justin, Mrs Hoskins and heaven knows who else, and pieced them into a totally wrong picture.'

'Put me right,' he prompted.

'I'm not a temp. I'm a linguist and a head-hunter. I manage the Paris bureau of the Harry Preston Euro Executive Consultancy.'

Callum's response wasn't quite what she expected. His eyebrows lowered in a frown she was beginning to know so well. 'Then your *man* friend is also your boss. Who's the opportunist, you or him?'

'Neither, not that it's any of your business. It's just something that—that developed. All I'm trying to make clear is that I don't need any hand-outs, nor do I starve myself to buy clothes as Mrs Hoskins seems to think. The gardener's granddaughter has done very nicely for herself!'

Indignation, frustration—whatever!—put magnificent fire into Gaby's eyes, but all Callum said was, 'That's torn it. I was hoping to hire you more permanently.'

'You won't catch me running around this place in a cap and pinny again,' she snapped.

'Now there's a picture to conjure up,' he murmured

provocatively, 'although I actually had something completely different in mind.'

'I'm not interested.'

'Reserve judgement, Gaby, just one more time.' Callum took her hand, pulled her to her feet and led her out of the dining-room. She followed because she hadn't any choice. Her vociferous protests died when they entered the great hall. It was the first time she'd seen it and she couldn't help but be impressed.

'It's magnificent,' she breathed, awed, as she looked at the lofty hammer-beam ceiling, the newly white-washed walls and the massive fireplace.

'It certainly has atmosphere, and so it should. Here's where my ancestors used to tear their meat apart with their bare hands and throw the bones into the straw under the table for the dogs to fight over.'

'Some things change for the better,' Gaby said. Their eyes met, they smiled at each other, and she was the one who felt compelled to break the contact. He was still holding her hand, and she was conscious enough of that. She found herself looking at the hovering kestrel in the Durand coat of arms carved in stone above the fireplace. A bird of prey poised to pounce. Involuntarily she looked again at Callum. She wondered if the prey felt as she did now. Too mesmerised to flee to safety.

Callum's hand tightened on hers. 'You're shivering.'

She shrugged. 'I'm glad that kestrel's in stone. It looks as though it means business.'

'Kestrels usually do.' He seemed amused, and glanced back at the coat of arms as he led her on. 'Perhaps I should cage it in with a bar-sinister to denote the illegitimate line's taken over.'

'They do say if you've got it, flaunt it,' Gaby replied lightly, not knowing quite what else to say.

Callum gave a shout of laughter that echoed around the ancient hall, and then he took her into the passage beyond. Gaby felt ridiculously pleased that she'd made him laugh like that, and she stopped feeling self-conscious about her hand clasped in his. It seemed right, somehow.

In fact, she felt strangely bereft when he took her into the room at the end of the corridor and released her. It was the library, long, oak-panelled and mellow, with lattice windows facing them and double french windows at the end. Callum opened them. 'A Victorian alteration, and for once a good one,' he said.

Gaby stood at his shoulder and found herself looking at a walled patio garden. 'It's lovely,' she said, and then turned round to study the room. Old bookcases, a massive desk, two wing-chairs and a sofa grouped around a fireplace, several telephones and lots of electronic equipment that curiously didn't seem incongruous. 'You work here,' she said.

'Most of the time. I also have an office in London I visit a couple of times a week, and occasionally there are field trips to study companies for myself. I don't believe in investing blind.' Callum took her arm and led her towards a graceful spiral staircase. 'Ladies first.'

Gaby began to climb, very conscious of her bare legs and Callum so close behind her. 'What's up here?' she asked.

'Gaby's room. I didn't know it when I had it prepared and this staircase installed for easy access from the library,' he explained in answer to the puzzled look she shot over her shoulder at him, 'but I hope that's what it becomes.'

The room she stepped into smelled freshly decorated. The ceiling had been recently painted white and

the old beams revarnished. Above the waist-high wain-
scoting the walls had new green and white striped
wallpaper. The curtains and carpet were new. The only
signs of antiquity were chests and boxes of all ages and
sizes in the middle of the room. The rest—a long desk
set before the latticed windows, a smaller desk with a
word processor, bookcases with drawers and cupboards
below, a row of filing cabinets—were spanking new.

Gaby hadn't known what to expect—a bed, perhaps,
for easy seduction—but she was more puzzled than
ever. 'What's this got to do with me?'

'I'm hoping you'll work here.' He anticipated her
protests by carrying on, 'I know, you don't need the
money. What if we called it a labour of love?'

'I don't know what you're talking about.'

Callum moved into the centre of the room and
touched one of the old chests with his foot. 'You love
Shorelands, don't you? Well, the manor is the heart of
it and all the family records are in these boxes. Ledgers,
diaries, household accounts, letters. Nearly three
hundred years of them. There are maps, sketches and
photographs as well. . .in fact, all the paper clutter the
Durands didn't know what to do with so they stuffed
them in the attics and forgot about them. The Hazletts
never bothered to clear out the attics either when they
left, so I think it's time somebody did something about
them.'

Gaby couldn't help but be intrigued, 'You mean
there's virtually a year by year account of manorial life
from the sixteenth century here? But that's fascinating!'

'I'd hoped you would think so,' Callum said. 'I had
two small guest rooms knocked into one to make a
very mundane-sounding records office. Gaby's room
sounds much more interesting.'

Callum was smiling at her in a way that made her

feel flustered, and she knew she had to keep a cool head. It wasn't easy. Her fingers were itching to get among those old family papers. She tried to sound nothing more than politely interested as she asked, 'There are personal letters, too, as well as accounts?'

'Family letters describing trips to town or abroad. Gossip letters from friends. Love-letters that will make your hair curl. The Durands are a passionate lot.'

He said 'are' not 'were', and his smile brought soft colour to her cheeks. She turned away, trying to laugh but not quite managing it. 'It sounds to me less of a labour of love and more of a labour of a lifetime. I've only got six weeks and I've other things to do.'

'You could make a start,' Callum coaxed. 'I want everything recorded and filed so that we know exactly what we've got and where to find it.

Gaby turned and faced him. 'Any temp could do the job for you. Why me?'

'You love Shorelands,' he repeated. 'You'd work with care and dedication, and those aren't always qualities one can hire. And we're compatible, that's important. I don't care to work with people I don't like around me.'

Compatible. . .the word lingered in Gaby's mind. Had they really come so far in such a short time, or was the antagonism still there, waiting to flare up at an unguarded moment? 'I'm supposed to be on holiday,' she said slowly.

Against her better judgement she was being swayed, and Callum was astute enough to know it. He was also clever enough not to push her too far. 'Come along whenever the mood takes you,' he suggested. 'You'll be welcome any time, and what you do really will be appreciated. What do you say, Gaby?'

'Yes,' she said, capitulating to a need to be here at

the manor with Callum. It wasn't what she'd returned to Shorelands for, quite the reverse, but her needs were changing, growing. . .

'That's my girl,' Callum said, smiling in a way that seemed reward enough itself. He must have seen the sudden doubt in her eyes, because his manner changed, became brisk. 'Are you ready to make a start now?'

'No.' She had to assert herself or Callum would take her over completely. 'I've got a date with my garden this morning.'

'All right, let's get to it.'

'I didn't mean you,' Gaby said hurriedly. 'Just me. I enjoy gardening.'

'And I enjoy your company,' Callum told her. 'I don't know about the gardening, but as you're helping me I feel honour bound to help you.'

'I doubt very much if you ever feel honour bound to do anything,' she retorted, again overwhelmed with the feeling he was playing some kind of game with her, 'or am I supposed to reserve judgement on that as well?'

'You're learning,' Callum said. 'I knew you would.'

CHAPTER EIGHT

IT WAS make believe and yet it was real. There was Callum stripped to his shorts digging out the roots of brambles and ivy, and here was she in halter top and shorts kneeling on a cushion he'd fetched from the sitting-room, while she weeded around a great cluster of white daisy-like chrysanthemums. His Jaguar was parked in the drive, and behind them her quaint Hansel and Gretel gatehouse drowsed in the sun.

Gaby sat back on her heels and looked round at the house. As a child she'd imagined it a place where magical things could happen. As a woman, she felt she'd been proved right. A couple of children, a cat and a dog, she mused dreamily, and everything would be absolutely perfect.

Then she realised how she was letting her happiness run away with her, how fatally easy it was to dupe herself into slipping from the real to the make believe. Guiltily she leaned forward to work again, her head bent to hide her blushing face.

'Gaby.'

She had to look at him. She couldn't pretend to be deaf. She peeled the gardening gloves from her hands to gain a little time, but her colour was still high when she sat back and replied, 'Yes?'

Callum studied her, then stuck his shovel in the earth, came over and lifted her to her feet. 'I thought so,' he said. 'You've had enough sun and work for one day. You flake out in the deck-chair and I'll get us some drinks.'

131

'I'll do that,' Gaby began, but he was leading her to the deck-chair still far back under the oak tree where she'd left it yesterday.

'And don't let me catch you falling asleep in the sun again,' Callum continued. 'You'll burn.'

'Then it was you who shifted me?'

'Who did you think it was, a woodwose?' He smiled and went away into the house.

Gaby sank into the deck-chair. So it had been Callum, not Justin, who'd lifted her into the shade yesterday, and it seemed he was still set on looking after her. She began to feel pampered. It was a nice feeling.

Callum came back carrying two long glasses filled with lemon barley and ice. He'd put on his shirt and he sat on the grass beside her. They both drank thirstily and then he said, 'Can you ride?'

'I used to.'

'That's good enough. Come to work for me in the morning, we'll have some lunch, then go for a ride along the beach in the afternoon,' he suggested. 'What do you think?'

'It sounds fine.' Gaby looked down at the ice melting in her glass. She was remembering how fiercely she used to yearn to be the girl by Justin's side when he went riding, and now it was to be with Callum. That was what she wanted, but she still felt a little tug at her heart. The old dream had gone, and yet in some strange way she still felt tied to it. She could only suppose loyalty survived when the love that inspired it was dead. She wished it wasn't so. It made her feel not quite—free.

Her mind jumped from Justin to Harry, the man who'd coloured all her thoughts in Paris and whom she couldn't even conjure up in black and white since she'd met Callum.

Callum—he was the catalyst. She looked at him and felt a different sort of tug at her heart. She couldn't imagine herself anywhere, or under any circumstances, where he would fade to little more than a half-remembered shadow. She was falling in love as a woman for the first time, and tomorrow they would be together. . .

Meanwhile, the rest of the day stretched emptily before her and she waited hopefully. If Callum felt the same as she did, he would suggest something. He wouldn't want the rest of the day lost, which it would be if they weren't together. Anticipation tingled pleasantly through her when he put down his empty glass and asked, 'What are you doing for the rest of the day?'

'Nothing special,' she replied, so he'd know her options were open. 'Perhaps laze a bit, walk a bit, swim a bit. Whatever takes my fancy.'

'Make sure there's plenty of lazing. You're inclined to overdo things.' Callum stood up. 'I'm invited to a lunchtime barbecue. It's a long-standing arrangement so I have to go. I wish I could take you, but it's not my party so it might be a bit awkward.'

Gaby hid her disappointment by stretching back in the deck-chair and closing her eyes. 'Thanks for the thought, but I doubt if I'd have the energy to get ready. Have fun.'

She could sense Callum looking down at her. She yearned for him to say something special or touch her, but all she got was a very ordinary, 'I'll see you tomorrow,' and then he was walking away. She heard the Jaguar start, and didn't open her eyes again until the sound of the engine was lost somewhere on the road to the manor. Emotionally she was still with him, and she didn't know what to do with the shell that was left. Time passed and she felt no inclination to get on with the day.

Gaby was staring round the garden, seeking inspiration and trying to summon up some vitality, when she heard another car. Not, as a few seconds of anxious listening told her, Callum's Jag returning, or even Mrs Hoskins' Mini. This was a sound from the past, and she wasn't surprised when Justin arrived in an updated model of the showy sports car he always used to drive. The top was folded back and he jumped out as she walked over to him.

He looked devastatingly handsome. His long black hair was windswept, he was smiling in a way that should have curled her toes but didn't, and he was as immaculately dressed as ever in superbly tailored cream trousers and shirt. A silk cravat was knotted at his throat, just as it always used to be, and Gaby had the curious feeling he was trapped in a time capsule of his own.

She hadn't thought she'd changed, but, the longer she looked at him, the more she realised how much she had. Nothing could have brought home more forcibly to her that Justin wasn't her beau ideal any longer. He was too boyish, and she might never have known it if he hadn't been totally eclipsed by his less perfect but altogether more manly half-brother.

Justin moved so confidently towards her, so certain of his visual appeal, that she felt an almost overwhelming compassion for him. Spoilt, pampered and adored all his life, no wonder he couldn't come to terms with the kind of competition Callum offered, or comprehend why he was losing out all round. He thought all Callum's power was in his money and he was wrong, so very wrong.

'I don't remember much about last night, but I gather I was pretty offensive,' Justin said, coming straight to the point. He raised her hand to his lips and kissed it, clever enough to let his lips linger while his eyes held hers. 'Forgive me, Gaby?'

She remembered her humiliation and wasn't to be won over so easily. 'You seemed to think I'd dressed up specially to flirt with you. I didn't.'

'I know. Callum's just got through telling me. The waitress didn't turn up, and you stepped in wearing the only black clothes you have with you.' Justin's eyes gleamed with sudden humour. 'I wish I had been right, though. You were a knock-out.'

Gaby pulled her hand out of his. 'I thought you couldn't remember.'

'How could I possibly forget that part of it? I was drunk, Gaby, not dead.'

She was amused, but she couldn't quite forgive him, nor did she entirely trust him. 'Did Callum send you over to apologise?'

Justin's sunny good humour vanished. 'No, he didn't. I don't need him to teach me my manners.'

'You could have fooled me last night.'

Gaby saw the swift flash of anger in his eyes, and saw it just as swiftly die. 'I suppose I deserve that. Let me make amends by taking you to dinner tonight. I'll pick you up at eight,' Justin said. 'I'll be as sober as a judge, I promise you. I don't make a habit of letting the side down.'

She began to shake her head, but he pressed harder, 'Oh, come on, Gaby. I'm due back in London tomorrow, and I can't take you out now because I promised I'd be at the Armstrongs' barbecue.'

So that was where Callum had rushed off to—Kate's! He hadn't breathed a word about that, but now she could understand why he couldn't take her with him. Naturally she and Kate had to be kept far apart. He could scarcely flirt with them both at the same time.

Hurt, Gaby said recklessly, 'Eight o'clock it is, then. I might even wear the black dress.'

'That's what I like, a girl who doesn't mind living dangerously,' Justin said, and laughed. He went to open the gates, climbed back into his car, and added, 'Promise it will be the black dress and I'll take you somewhere really special.'

'It's a promise,' she replied, full of simulated gaiety because she had so much hurt to hide.

Justin laughed and drove out through the gates. Gaby went slowly to close them, and all she could think of was Callum and Kate. . .Kate and Callum. She could only mock herself for being deluded into believing she could find happiness here at Shorelands, when she knew of old there could only be hurt.

She was only safe with Harry. No greats highs with him, perhaps, but no desperate lows either. She was trying to persuade herself to settle for him when the whisper in her heart started up again, and she knew she could do no such thing. If her heart was going to break again at Shorelands, she would see it through. She'd never know any peace if she ran away.

Determinedly, Gaby pulled herself together and drove into Shevingham, where she lunched at the Fisherman's Dream and chatted away to John as though she hadn't a care in the world. If he'd heard any gossip about the dinner party at Shorelands he didn't mention it, and for that she was grateful.

Later on in the afternoon she went swimming, and by the time she returned to the gatehouse in the evening she had a healthy-looking tan. After she'd bathed she studied her reflection in the old cheval-glass

her bedroom and thought it a pity she'd promised to
ar black. White would set off her tan better. Still,
e would sweep her hair up as she did for Harry, and
ar her pearl earrings with the tiny tear-like drops.
e earrings were the only genuine jewellery she
ssessed and they would flatter her tan.

She prepared herself slowly, leisurely, her bruised
de demanding she make the most of herself, and
en she was finished she was pleased. The dusky
eshadow made her eyes larger and more luminous,
e pink gloss on her lips was sexy, the earrings
ivered with her every movement, and the unclut-
ed black dress was the last word in sophisticated
ic. All that was lacking was the glow of excited
ticipation a date with Callum would have given her,
t she doubted if Justin would notice that.

He called for her promptly, looking so impossibly
ndsome in a dark suit and white shirt that if she
dn't met Callum she'd have thought all her dreams
d come true. He whistled, saying appreciatively, 'I
ought I'd miss the sexy pinny and cap, but you look
perb.'

Ever the opportunist, he bent to kiss her, but Gaby
artly turned her head so that his lips landed on her
eek. It was an obvious snub and she knew it rankled,
t what could she do? She didn't know how to love
e man and give her lips to another. She simply didn't
ve the Durand brothers' facility to play those sort of
mes.

'So I'm still not entirely forgiven,' Justin said, leading
r out to his open sports car. 'I'll have to see what I
n do about that.'

To save answering, Gaby busied herself with wrap-
ng a scarf around her head. It was a fine evening,
th the sun reluctant to sink in the scarcely darkening

sky and the salty sea breeze hardly ruffling the tops of the tall trees. Justin drove in his old flashy style, all accelerator and brakes, but he seemed to know what he was doing and she was just beginning to relax when he stopped at Shevingham's only crossing.

A girl with a dog was passing in front of the car, a freckle-faced blonde whom Gaby recognised as Amanda Highfield, Sam's secretary. She also recognised the look of longing and envy in Amanda's eyes. There'd been many times when she, too, must have had that particular look on her face when Justin drove by with a girl by his side.

Poor Amanda, Gaby thought with fellow feeling, and would willingly have changed places with her. She saw Justin raise a hand in a careless salute which Amanda half returned, then she was past and they were driving on. Justin began to talk about his experiences in the States, and also told her a little of his own publishing company in England. He was charming, a totally different person from the drunk who'd humiliated her last night, and Gaby couldn't help but wonder if it was Callum who brought out the worst in him.

Justin took her to a nightclub on the outskirts of Norwich, where he'd booked a table set back from the band and dance-floor. They both ordered gazpacho followed by lobster thermidor. While they were eating the chilled soup, he asked, 'Sam Gibson tells me you're hedging about selling the gatehouse. Is that to push up the price?'

'No.'

'Oh, come on, Gaby! We both know Callum wants it and can afford to pay any price you ask,' Justin said.

'I'm not into extortion,' she replied coolly. 'Nobody seems to believe me, but the truth is I just haven't finally decided what to do about the house yet.'

'Sell it to me.'

Gaby stared at him in amazement. 'You—but why? You're used to the manor. I can't see you being happy in the gardener's gatehouse!'

'Too much of a come-down, do you mean?' Justin shrugged. 'Times change. It's the only way I'm likely to have an independent stake in Shorelands. I can't keep bowing and scraping to my brother—if he is my brother.'

Gaby was once more overwhelmed with compassion for him. It didn't take much imagination to guess how hideous it must be for Justin having to keep on the right side of Callum if he wanted to keep in touch with what should have been his birthright and inheritance. There was nothing she could say about that which wouldn't sound trite and so she asked, 'What do you mean, "if he is your brother"?'

Justin had finished eating and he toyed with his wine glass. 'The Durands have never been saints. He could just as easily be the son of some other Durand bastard from way back, and I think that's just what he is. If he was really my father's son he would have proved it, and he never has. No, he's just pretending to be something he isn't.'

It hurt Gaby to think of Callum as any kind of a pseud, and she asked, 'Why do you go along with him, then? If you didn't accept him as your brother, nobody else would, and where's the sense in staying at Shorelands if it's painful?'

Justin shot her a disgruntled look as though he resented her questions. 'I was hoping Callum would have enough family feeling to do the right thing and sell Shorelands back to me. I've had time to raise more finance. I could meet his price, but he's too much in love with being Squire Durand.'

Gaby felt compelled to say, 'I don't think that's true. In fact, I'm sure it isn't.'

His hand came across the table and touched hers. He gave the smile that no longer had the power to devastate her and murmured, 'Gaby, darling, I thought you were on my side. Surely you're not yet another rat ready to desert the sinking ship?'

Gaby, hating to be disloyal to Justin, discovered she couldn't be disloyal to Callum, either. Floundering, she could only stick to the truth. 'I'm neither your darling nor a rat, and your own particular ship sank before ever Callum came on the scene,' she retorted indignantly. 'It was your own father who sold you out, not Callum.'

'If you must be precise, yes, but it was Callum who stopped me recouping my losses,' he pointed out. 'He didn't need Shorelands, so why the hell did he buy it?'

'He fell in love with the place, and that's not exactly hard to understand, is it?'

Justin laughed, a mirthless sound. 'If you believe that, you'll believe anything. Callum's an opportunist, an exploiter. That's how he made his money, and a leopard doesn't change its spots.'

Gaby felt a quiver of unease, but then she remembered Justin had good reason to be bitter, and she didn't want to reveal her own feelings for Callum by defending him too obviously. She fell silent—not that Justin noticed, because the waiter was serving the second course. As they began to eat again he seemed to have got himself in hand because he said mildly, 'Sorry, Gaby, I don't want to involve you in my problems, but I would appreciate first option on the gatehouse.'

She let a minute or so pass before she asked, 'Why do you think Callum bought Shorelands, then?'

Justin stared at her hard, then shrugged. 'Sometimes when I'm mad I say more than I intend. Let's just forget about it. There are better things to talk about—like you.'

She accepted the change of subject with relief, thinking it was only Justin's bitterness that had made him snipe at Callum, a bitterness he was already regretting. Perhaps there was hope yet that the brothers, if brothers they were, would find a way of getting along amicably together.

There was a slight disturbance, and whatever pleasure Gaby might have wrested from the evening died. Callum and Kate were being shown to a table adjacent to theirs. Justin didn't seem at all surprised. He waved a hand in casual greeting and carried on talking. Gaby's eyes met Callum's and he gave the briefest nod. She had the distinct impression he was angry at seeing her with Justin, but that was ridiculous when he was with Kate!

Annoyed, she found a sparkle that had been lacking before, and gave a very good impression of a girl enjoying herself as though she hadn't a care in the world. Justin responded just as she'd hoped. She hadn't a clue what they were talking or laughing about, determined only that Callum would never guess how much it hurt her to see him with Kate.

The few glances she managed to steal across the room showed her that Kate was just as engrossed with Callum. She was wearing floating sea-green gauze over silk, making Gaby wish she'd gone for femininity instead of sophistication herself. Her head, which never ached, began to ache now. It was an effort to stay sparkling when she just wanted to crawl away and sink into misery.

Justin danced with her between courses, and once

when she couldn't resist looking at Callum she met his eyes. She smiled, because that was the natural thing to do. His flinty blue eyes didn't soften and he didn't smile back. She didn't want to crawl away now, she just wanted to die. He might at least have thought her important enough to merit some kind of acknowledgement.

When she and Justin returned to their table it was with the greatest difficulty that she got through the rum babas. She wished she'd ordered something lighter, but her spirit wouldn't let her plead a headache so they could leave. Justin showed no inclination to hurry. He'd scarcely touched his wine, but he was relaxed and enjoying himself.

Her misery, Gaby told herself severely, was her own fault. It shouldn't hurt so much to see Callum with Kate. She had no right to expect anything from him. All right, so she'd fooled herself into thinking they'd become close. She knew better now.

While they were drinking their coffee the band struck up a romantic waltz. Not for the world could Gaby stop her eyes going to Callum, and she saw him stand up and offer his hand to Kate. Lucky Kate, Gaby thought. It had always been lucky Kate. She looked back to see Justin standing and smiling at her. He led her on to the crowded dance-floor and took her into his arms, and all she could feel was a terrible sadness that once a childhood dream faded it couldn't be revived.

Justin was like an outgrown toy she still had a certain soft spot for but no longer wanted. Worse than that, even if she could turn back the clock she wouldn't. Callum's grip on her was too absolute for that. Gaby found herself wondering wearily just what the future

eld for her. Certainly not Harry. Callum had killed
hat relationship stone-dead, too.

There was a brief pause in the first of a medley of
waltzes before the second began. The bandmaster
urned to the microphone and said, 'Change partners,
lease,' and then struck up the next tune. They were
ext to Callum and Kate. Gaby looked wildly to see
who was on their other side, but then Justin was
waltzing away with Kate and she was in Callum's arms.

She didn't look up. There was nothing but a broad
xpanse of shoulder facing her, and it took all her
trength not to lean her head against it. Callum's hand
was firm on her waist, and his closeness took her breath
way. She felt weightless, dizzy with the vicarious thrill
f a few minutes' stolen happiness. It lasted right up
ntil Callum said, 'I thought you knew Justin wasn't
ny good for you.'

His tone was curt, accusing, and it stirred rebellion
within Gaby. Her head came up proudly and she
eplied, 'I can manage my own affairs, thank you.'

'How many affairs do you manage at any one time?'
e asked coldly.

The implication brought the blood rushing to Gaby's
heeks. She turned her head away from his searching
yes, too hurt and furious to speak. The music stopped,
nother change of partners was requested and she
urned thankfully to some anonymous man who began
o dance with her.

When it was over and she was back at the table she
oticed Justin's mood had also changed. His eyes were
littering dangerously, although his smile was as perfect
s ever when he said, 'I have to make an early start for
London tomorrow, if you don't mind leaving now?'

She was on her feet immediately, deliberately keep-
ng her eyes away from Callum's table. There wasn't

the slighest need for her to be polite to him and, as Kate scarcely deigned to notice her, there was no need to bother about her, either.

She was used to the controlled recklessness of Justin's driving as they returned to Shorelands, but she sensed his nerves were as strung out as hers. He didn't say why, but they both had to struggle out of their own thoughts to make an effort to say something now and again.

Perhaps he'd discovered after playing fast and loose with Kate for years that he loved her after all, perhaps as much as she loved Callum. Poor me, poor Justin, she thought, and yet she was certain he'd known Kate and Callum would be there tonight. Everybody seemed to know what was going on except herself. In forty-eight hours her world had been turned upside-down and she didn't know how to put it right. She'd only learned what real misery was.

Gaby was thankful when they reached the gatehouse. She wanted to be alone, but as Justin helped her from the car politeness made her say, 'It's been a lovely evening. Would you like to round it off with coffee?'

'I'm depending on it.' Justin seemed almost his own self again, but there was enough moonlight to show her his smile was a parody of the real thing. Yes, he was suffering, and once more she was swamped with fellow feeling.

She unlocked the front door and told him to make himself comfortable in the sitting-room. He seemed too restless for that and followed her into the kitchen. As she put on the percolator, he said, 'What about something stronger?'

'Not for me. I haven't got anything, anyway.'

'I wonder. . .' Justin disappeared into the walk-in pantry and came out clutching a half-full bottle of brandy. 'He who hides can surely find,' he declared, grinning at her, and went straight to the cabinet where the glasses were kept and took out two.

Gaby put one back. 'Not for me,' she said firmly. She'd known the bottle was in the pantry, but thought it had been left there by the squatters. It had seemed unlikely the char was a secret tippler or she'd have taken it with her when Sam fired her. She remembered Callum's angry reference to Justin's 'love-nest' and continued coldly, 'You've been using the gatehouse, haven't you?'

Justin shrugged. 'I knew you wouldn't mind.'

Gaby did mind, very much. The char must have known what Justin was up to and, through her, Sam. Even Amanda. That would account for the freckle-faced blonde being so uncomfortable when Gaby and Sam had discussed the gatehouse and Justin. Perhaps she was one of the women who'd been here. Sam should have stopped it, though. He was her agent and, she'd thought, her friend.

Justin was watching the play of expressions across her face as he drank his brandy. He poured himself another and said, 'You look shocked. I'd no idea you were such a little prude.'

'I'd no idea you hit the bottle so often,' she snapped. 'You're never going to regain what you've lost that way!'

The brandy must have mellowed Justin because he didn't get angry, he just tutted, 'Steady, Gaby, you're beginning to sound like the bastard, and I've had as much of that as I can stand.'

She'd been pouring her coffee with a none-too-steady hand, but she rounded on him furiously, 'Don't call Callum that!'

Justin whistled. 'So that's the way the land lies! I should have guessed he'd win you over, too.'

'Don't be ridiculous!' Perhaps it was the realisation that he wasn't being ridiculous at all that took the steam out of Gaby and made her say wearily, 'Oh, don't let's fight. Put that wretched brandy down and have some coffee, Justin.'

'All right.'

Gaby was surprised and relieved as she carried the coffees into the sitting-room, and they began to talk of other things. He sat a little apart from her on the sofa, but he'd brought the bottle in with him too, and when he'd half drunk his coffee he filled the cup with brandy, and then again.

She wished she could be angry with him, but she just felt so sorry. 'Justin, you're ruining yourself over Shorelands. If you can't bear to see Callum in your place, go away and stay away.'

'I can't. I've got one last shot to play.'

Gaby frowned. 'What do you mean?'

Justin was more than half drunk now, but he managed to look as handsome as ever as he tapped the side of his nose to indicate secrecy. 'Mustn't let Kate get to hear about it,' he said.

He was talking in riddles and, to judge by the level of the brandy, he wasn't going to get any better. Gaby stood up. 'I'll get my car keys and run you home.'

'What a good little Girl Guide you are,' he murmured, leaning back and closing his eyes.

Gaby took the bottle into the kitchen, poured the last of the brandy away, and made him a strong cup of coffee. When she returned Justin was stretched out on the sofa fast asleep. She didn't want him spending the night here. The neighbourhood was probably already

fe with rumours about them. She put the coffee on
he table, bent to rouse him, then paused.

Why the devil should she worry? Callum already
hought the worst of her, and he was out somewhere
ith Kate. Throwing Justin out smacked too much of
timidation, and if that was the way Callum worked
e was going to come unstuck with her. Gaby bent
orward again, but it was to loosen Justin's collar and
ake off his tie and shoes. She fetched a blanket to
over him and then she went to bed.

Callum could make what he liked of that.

CHAPTER NINE

THE dream was delicious. Callum was stroking her rumpled hair back from her face. He touched her face. Gaby smiled, turned her head and kissed his palm. His hand moved on, tracing the line of her neck and bare shoulder. His lips followed his fingers and she gave a little moan of pleasure as he kissed the precise spot where her neck and shoulder joined.

'Gaby, you little witch,' he breathed, no dream at all but real.

Her eyes flew open and she recoiled. The night had been hot and she was only covered by a sheet. She grabbed it and pulled it up to her neck. 'Justin!' she exclaimed.

He smiled. 'Who else?'

She couldn't tell him. She could only protest, 'Get out of my bedroom!'

Justin stayed right where he was, lying across her and propped up on his elbow. 'You don't mean that, not after the way you've led me on.'

'I didn't. I thought I was dreaming.' Gaby, shocked, stared about the room as though trying to get her bearings. She felt so cheated, so terribly sad, that her mind wouldn't function properly. Dazedly she saw the sun was streaming in the window, so it was much later than when she normally woke.

Trying to blink herself into proper awareness, she looked again at Justin. He seemed to have showered. His hair was damp and his white shirt was open over his trousers. He looked incredibly handsome, but his

ensuality had no effect on her. She just felt like
weeping because he wasn't Callum.

'A girl like you doesn't have to dream,' Justin
breathed, his lips finding that vulnerable spot on her
shoulder again. 'For you, things happen for real.'

Her flesh, yearning for Callum, was revolted, and
she pushed him away in panic. 'Stop it, Justin. I wasn't
dreaming about you!'

He drew back, unable to mask his surprise, and then
his winning smile spread over his face. 'I could soon
change that. . .'

As his voice trailed away suggestively, Gaby
snapped, 'Just go away. I let you stay over because I
had no choice, not because I fancied you.'

Justin bent to kiss her bare shoulder again. When
she shoved him away he spread his hands pacifically
and got off the bed. 'All right, all right, so you like to
tease. Just don't push it too far. I'm not exactly hard
up for a woman.'

He went out, leaving Gaby so angry that any linger-
ing sympathy she felt for him died. She couldn't believe
that anybody could be so egotistical, and as she recalled
Callum's remarks of the night before she decided he
wasn't much better, either. Both of them appeared to
think they could say what they liked to the gardener's
granddaughter, which meant both of them needed
putting right.

Gaby stayed where she was until she heard Justin's
car drive away, then she jumped out of bed. For a
moment she stood, irresolute. By returning to
Shorelands to free herself for Harry, she'd become
enmeshed in a situation she couldn't have foreseen.
Both Justin and Callum wanted to buy the gatehouse,
and any personal interest they had in her appeared to
stem from a need to spite the other.

If she had any sense she'd turn the gatehouse over to Sam Gibson to sell and return to the job which now appeared to be her entire future. But she was angry, too angry to consider what was sensible. She hadn't made this situation, but she wasn't going to run away from it. She would see it through—if only to prove to Callum and Justin that she was neither a pawn nor a bimbo, but somebody they would both regret having tangled with.

It was in this martial frame of mind that Gaby arrived at the manor an hour later and stalked through the ancient passages to the library. She tapped on the door and walked in without awaiting an invitation. She wasn't a hired hand and she had no intention of being servile.

Callum was talking into a phone, his eyes on the messages flashing up on a computer. The day was cooler, the sun not yet having broken through a layer of low-flying clouds, and Callum was dressed pretty much as she was in jeans, shirt and sweater.

He looked—Gaby didn't want to think about how he looked. Her treacherous flesh might weaken. She might find herself wondering what it would be like to have the right to walk straight into his arms and stay there until all the pain and anguish drained away. She found to her horror that she was actually walking towards him, when he turned his head towards her.

He studied her so carefully, so assessingly, that Gaby stopped short. It was all there in that look, how very much in control he was, how quickly he could have her floundering. Well, not this time! Her chin came up defiantly. He noted that, too, put down the phone and pressed a button that killed the computer. 'Good morning, Gaby,' he said.

So they were to be civil, were they? She didn't feel

at all civil. She ignored his greeting and retorted, 'You
and I have to get a few things straight.'

'I think we do.' Callum indicated a chair beside his
desk.

Gaby sat on it, then wished she hadn't. He didn't sit
on his own chair, but propped himself on the edge of
his desk, overpoweringly close and looking down at
her. Mentally she gave him top points for manoeuvring
himself into the dominant position, a good business
tactic, but she soldiered on, 'About last night—one
more nasty remark and you can get somebody else to
sort out the Durand records.'

'Last night was a mistake, and I'm sorry. I realised it
as soon as I saw how much I hurt you. I don't make a
practice of repeating mistakes, Gaby.'

She stared up at him dumbfounded. He'd pulled the
carpet out from under her feet, and yet he hadn't
explained why he felt her morals, or lack of them, were
any of his business, anyway. She was so irritated that,
perversely, now that she was vindicated she didn't want
to be. 'Justin spent the night at the gatehouse,' she
said. 'You must know that.'

'I know you didn't sleep with him. That's all that
matters.'

Gaby's heart began to beat in a painfully hopeful
way, and colour tinged her cheeks as she asked, 'How
could you know that?'

'Justin doesn't sulk and slam around when he's
scored, and that's just how he was before he left for
London.'

Gaby's hope died. Scored, she thought with revulsion—that was all Callum and Justin were interested
in, scoring points off each other! To rattle him, she
retorted, 'If it had happened, it might have been more
than simply scoring.'

'Not with Justin.'

He spoke with such assurance that she could have
slapped him. She didn't want him to be right, and it
didn't help to know that he was. She could only come
back to her original grievance and protest, 'It's still
none of your business, and I don't see why it should
matter to you anyway.'

For the first time Callum hesitated. After a few
seconds he said, 'I don't want you to be hurt. I
feel. . .responsible. . .for you while you're at
Shorelands.'

Gaby didn't want his responsibility, she wanted his
love—and if he loved her, he'd know he was the only
one who could hurt her. *Was* hurting her. She could
only defend herself with anger, and she snapped,
'You're sounding like the squire again.'

His lips twisted into a rueful smile. 'I guessed that
was coming. Don't be angry with me, Gaby. I want us
to be friends.'

She didn't know what to say. Right was on her side,
but somehow he'd defeated her. Gaby could only
blame herself for being stupid enough to stay so close
to him. She knew—and how she knew!—what funny
things happened to her when he was within touching
distance. They were happening now. The tingling
pulses, the overactive heart, the need to read more
into his words than he actually meant.

It wasn't easy, but she stood up and moved away.
From somewhere she summoned up her brisk business
voice to tell him, 'Friends, sure, I'll go for that. Why
not? But one of the things I wanted to get straight is
why I'm willing to sort out the Durand records. It's
pure self-interest. I want to know more about my own
family, and the Warrens must be mentioned in the
household accounts.'

Callum stood up too, but he didn't come towards her. 'I was afraid it might be that,' he said, and turned away.

Gaby was walking towards the spiral staircase, but he stopped, hoping he'd explain himself. He didn't. The phone rang and he moved round the desk to answer it. She walked on and up the staircase, feeling heated.

Callum didn't want her—not for the right reasons, anyway—but he never quite let her go, either. Fresh bitterness surged through Gaby as it dawned on her that, although it was Justin who had the reputation as a womaniser, he could learn a trick or two from his more subtle but infinitely more dangerous illegitimate brother.

She tried to absorb herself in her task, which would have been fascinating under different circumstances, but she found it very difficult to separate herself emotionally from Callum, and her mind kept wandering. She sifted through the oldest chest, found that the earliest document was dated 1696, and began a hand-written catalogue.

Later on, when she'd written a brief description of each document and was certain everything was chronologically correct, the information would be tapped into the computer. Meanwhile, she also had to organise a filing system. If she was going to do the job properly—and she didn't know any other way to work—most of her holiday would vanish in this room.

She couldn't think of a more masochistic way of keeping in contact with Callum, but it beat not seeing him at all. If her heart was going to break, some distant tomorrow would be soon enough. She just wasn't strong enough right now.

Around mid-morning Mrs Hoskins brought her

coffee and also tried to give her a ten-pound note. Gaby pushed it away. 'Put it in a charity box,' she insisted. 'I have an extremely well-paid job and I don't need the cash. I only helped out on Saturday night as a favour.' She touched the pile of documents she was working on and added, 'I'm not doing this for cash, either, but to learn what I can about my own family history.'

'Are you thinking of staying at Shorelands, after all?' Mrs Hoskins asked.

Gaby's heart lurched. She was finding it very hard to think of anything else. 'No,' she replied shortly.

'That's a pity. You seem to belong here, just like Mr Callum. Some of us do, you know, and there isn't anything we can do about it. We're just not happy anywhere else. You think about that before you do anything hasty.' Mrs Hoskins patted Gaby's shoulder in a motherly way and sedately left the room, leaving Gaby staring after her in consternation. If she couldn't convince the housekeeper she didn't want to stay at Shorelands, whom could she convince?

That question was still revolving in her brain when Callum came up at one o'clock and asked, 'How's it going?'

'Oh, it's fascinating stuff,' she said breezily. 'Just look at this map of Shorelands dated 1696. See. . .the manor's the only building marked, no tenant farms or anything, and the estate was almost all woodland. What a pity only patches of woods have survived. It must have been lovely then, with the deer running wild and. . .'

Gaby's voice trailed away. Callum was leaning over her to study the map, his hand coming down on her shoulder so that her whole world seemed to shrink to the warmth and excitement of that simple contact. He was so close that she could feel his breath on her cheek as he asked, 'What would you like, Gaby, complete reforestation? That's unrealistic, I'm afraid. Farmland is necessary to support the estate.'

'Yes, of course, but I hope you'll protect surviving woods and replace any trees that are lost naturally.'

She felt so strongly about it that she turned her face to his, her enthusiasm glowing in her huge eyes. Callum stared at her, and for a few crazy seconds she thought he was going to kiss her, then he straightened up and stepped away. Gaby was seared with a sense of loss that scarcely lessened when he said abruptly, 'You don't have to worry about any more woods being cleared. That's one wavelength we share.'

Gaby was pondering miserably on all the wavelengths they didn't share when he dropped a bundle of letters on her desk and stunned her by saying, 'These are the letters from Crispin Durand to my mother proving my paternity. You can file them away as my contribution to the Durand records.'

Gaby's soft lips parted in amazement. 'But I could read them. . .'

Callum shrugged. 'Feel free. It's a simple enough story. Crispin had an affair with my mother while he was separated from his wife. According to these letters, he intended marrying her when the divorce was finalised. She changed her name to Durand in anticipation so that I'd be born with the right surname. You could say we were stuck with it when he was reconciled with his wife and conveniently forgot about us. Justin was born a couple of years later. My mother never sued, she just set about supporting herself and me.'

Gaby stared at the letters. They were prosaically kept together with an elastic band, and there seemed so few of them to contain so much drama, however

matter-of-factly Callum related it. She didn't want to
pry, but she had to ask, 'Didn't your mother tell you
who your father was?'

'She died of peritonitis when I was three. My grand-
mother brought me up. She just said my father was a
married man who'd returned to his wife. Since he
didn't want to know about me, I didn't feel the slightest
need to know about him. It was only after I met Kate
and found out about Shorelands and Justin that she
gave me the letters. Even then I wouldn't have got
involved if——' for the first time Callum hesitated '——
if circumstances had been different.'

Gaby desperately wanted to know what those circumstances were, but it seemed his confidences were
at an end. She pushed her luck a little by asking, 'Why
haven't you shown Justin the letters?'

'I don't need to justify myself to Justin.'

His arrogance took Gaby's breath away. When she
thought it over she couldn't really blame him, although
she suggested, 'He'd find it easier to accept you if he
was certain you were his brother.'

'He's certain. He just prefers to resent me.'

'Then why do you put up with him?'

'I was giving him what he denied me—a fair innings.
It's just about over unless his attitude changes drasti-
cally. He wasn't in any doubt about that when he left
for London this morning, so it's up to him now.' Callum
saw the concerned expression on her face and his own
softened. 'Come on, you need your lunch and we'll
have Mrs Hoskins chasing us if we hang about here any
longer.'

As they went down the stairs and began the long
trek to the other end of the house, Gaby said in a
troubled voice, 'Justin wants to buy the gatehouse, but
if he can't get on with you surely he'd be better off

away from Shorelands altogether? His resentment would only fester if he was in the gatehouse and you in the manor.'

'So that's his game now, is it?' Callum mused, but he didn't seem at all surprised.

'What do you mean?' she asked, recalling with a sinking feeling Justin's remark about having one last card to play.

'Justin hasn't any intention of living in the gatehouse. His ideas are much too grand for that. He's aiming at a quick profit by reselling to me.'

'Oh.' Gaby felt betrayed, even though she no longer loved Justin.

They were walking through the great hall, but Callum stopped, put his hands on her shoulders and turned her to face him. 'Promise me, Gaby, that before you make any final decision on the gatehouse you'll talk to me first.'

'I promise,' she heard herself saying, although she knew her judgement might be warped. When Callum touched her, she'd promise anything, and perhaps he knew it. . .

Neither of them spoke again until they were in the breakfast parlour. The sun had broken through the clouds and the room was bright and welcoming. So was the selection of cold meats, salads and fruit set out for them. As they helped themselves, Callum asked, 'What would you do with Shorelands if it were yours, Gaby?'

She was so surprised that she blinked at him. He smiled and murmured, 'That's my little owl.'

There was a teasing note in his voice, almost a caress. It couldn't be, of course, and so she ignored the remark and stuck to the question. 'I'd stop poisoning the land and river with chemicals and switch to organic farming. It's less convenient and more expensive, but

there are enough people prepared to pay more for
healthy food to make it viable.'

Callum poured white wine into her glass and invited,
'Tell me about it.'

Gaby, the daughter of ecologists, needed no second
invitation. She spoke for twenty impassioned minutes
while he watched her with a half-smile on his face.
Finally she broke off, admitting ruefully, 'I could go on
all day.'

'I could listen all day.'

'You're teasing me.'

'I'm not.'

Gaby flushed a little, wanting so much to believe him
that she felt vulnerable again and needed to defend
herself with mockery. 'Phooey! You probably think
I'm some kind of nut.'

'No, a kindred spirit,' he said deliberately. 'No
chemicals have been used at Shorelands since I took
over.'

Impulsively Gaby reached out and covered his hand
with hers. 'Callum, that's marvellous. I thought——'

'Yes?' he prompted. 'What did you think?'

'That you'd go for the quick and easy profit. Most
people do. I'm sorry, I made a snap judgement and I
was wrong.'

'That makes us even.' He saw the puzzlement on her
face and explained, 'I made a snap judgement about
you once, and I was never more glad to be wrong.'

Gaby almost gasped, thinking he could only be
referring to the contemptuous way he'd linked her with
Justin's love-nest. If he was glad to be proved wrong,
that could only imply he was interested in her himself.
No, that couldn't be. He had Kate. Hopelessly mixed
up, and suddenly very self-conscious, she withdrew her

hand from his, wondering wherever she'd got the nerve to touch him in the first place.

He said quizzically, 'You're not the sort of girl to play around when you're already involved, are you, Gaby?'

Dumbly she shook her head, unable to explain that she wasn't involved in the way he thought she was. It would only seem as though she was eager to make herself available, and she had·too much pride for that. She was aware of how closely Callum was watching her and dared not meet his eyes, afraid he would read her thoughts. She was frantically trying to think of something innocuous to say to break the lengthening silence when he asked abruptly, 'How long is Preston going to leave you on your own like this?'

Gaby's nerves were so strung out that she jumped. 'I don't know. He's in Italy at the moment. I suppose I'll hear from him in a fortnight or so.'

'A fortnight,' he repeated. 'I suppose I can keep you safe at Shorelands for a fortnight, but I wouldn't guarantee any longer.'

Safe from whom? Himself? Her much-tried heart began to thump against her ribcage, but again she told herself she must be misunderstanding him. There was a far more obvious explanation. . . Justin. The rivalry between the brothers seemed to spill over everywhere. Neither really wanted her, or wanted the other to have her, either. Incensed, she retorted, 'I can keep myself safe, thank you. If Justin wants to get drunk next weekend, he can do so by himself.'

'He won't. I told you, remember, that he doesn't make a habit of it. He's much too concerned with his looks and the impression he's making. By next weekend he'll be over his upsets. He's had a hell of a weekend and it's not going to get any better if he stays in England. I've advised him to return to the States where his looks, accent and charm go down big. He'll probably marry a rich widow, buy up half a State and found a new dynasty. It was what he should have done in the first place instead of coming back here.'

Gaby could scarcely believe what she was hearing. Callum sounded as though he was talking about a stranger, not his brother. There were so many things she wanted to say, but the first that came out was, 'But he's got his own publishing company here!'

'Not for much longer,' Callum contradicted. 'It was failing when he bought it and he hasn't managed to turn it around.'

'Surely you could help?'

'I wouldn't be in business long if I threw good money after bad. I've had one of my men check the company out. There's nothing in it to justify investment.'

Her indignation rose and spilled over. 'This is different. It's not business, it's family.'

Callum gave a not very pleasant smile. 'How would you feel if the only time you were permitted to be family was when it came to writing a cheque?'

Gaby was silenced, but not for long. 'You can scarcely expect him to be all sweetness and light when you stopped him getting Shorelands back!'

'So your loyalty is still with him.' Callum leaned back in his chair, and she felt he was separating himself from her by more than distance. After a moment, he added, 'I was hoping it wouldn't be.'

'It's not a question of loyalty, but of objectivity,' Gaby snapped, hating this inhuman side of Callum. 'Not content with Shorelands, you also took Kate.'

'No, I didn't,' he said calmly. 'It's what everybody else thought, but not Justin, and certainly not me. I learned a long time ago the difference between a woman who's interested in me and one who's interested in what she can *get* from me.'

Gaby shook her head in bewilderment and ran a distracted hand through her hair. 'I don't understand. I thought. . .'

As he watched her, Callum's mouth softened. 'Poor Gaby, you've been so intent on seeing me as the villain of the piece.'

'No, it's not that. Oh, I wish you'd explain!'

'It's not a very pretty story. Kate and Justin have had an on-off affair for years. It was "off" when she met me and brought me to Shorelands. She'd no idea Justin was negotiating to buy the place back by private treaty. He and his backers kept very quiet about it for fear of being gazumped. Well, I was the one who did the gazumping. Justin was furious with Kate, and she was furious with him for keeping her in the dark.'

Callum paused, lifted the wine bottle, but when Gaby shook her head he put it down again without refilling his own glass. Then he continued, 'I've come to the conclusion that they're the sort of couple who can't live happily with or without each other. Sad, but it happens. The only thing that can unite them for any length of time is an outside force—in this case, me. They hatched up a scheme for Kate to use her feminine wiles to persuade me to sell Shorelands to Justin. It was a wild card, but the only one they had to play. . .and Kate is a beautiful woman.'

'Yes,' Gaby agreed, learning again what real pain was. It was the pain, linked with jealousy, that made her ask, 'How far was Kate prepared to go for Justin's sake.'

'As far as she had to,' Callum replied calmly.

'And Justin was prepared to let her?' When Callum nodded, she murmured, 'Poor Kate.'

'You're very charitable to Kate. What about poor me?'

'You're obviously very capable of looking after yourself. If you'd figured all this out, it was rotten of you to lead them on.'

Callum's lips twisted. 'No, naïve. I was hoping that if I gave Justin enough time to get to know me there'd be enough brotherly feeling for him to call a halt, or at least be honest with me. Now I know we'll always be strangers, and always on opposite sides of the fence. You, Gaby, are the catalyst who's brought it all to a head.'

'Me?' she protested. 'I've only been here a few days, and I've been very careful not to get mixed up in your feud.'

'You couldn't help yourself. It was on Friday when Justin came down that I told him I wouldn't invest in his publishing company, then you turned up just as he needed a boost to his ego. After that embarrassing scene he made at the dinner party, I made the mistake of warning him off you.' Callum paused and smiled at her in a way that seemed so tender she almost believed he truly cared for her, and that she wasn't merely a pawn in a game that had been none of her making. 'That, of course, was a mistake,' Callum went on. 'I didn't know then that my little owl had her head screwed on properly. I just didn't want you being— used. All I succeeded in doing was whipping up his interest, and Kate did the rest.'

Gaby, uncomprehending but still putting first things first, protested, 'I am not your little owl, and I don't see what Kate has to do with it.'

Callum smiled. 'You're not strictly beautiful, Gaby, but you pack your own brand of dynamite, and Kate's shrewd enough to know it. The fool Justin made of himself over you on Saturday night precipitated her into making a big play for me, knowing that if she could seduce me into believing I didn't want Shorelands, Justin would return to heel. I was unresponsive, and she thought it was because I was so mad at Justin for ruining the dinner party.'

He stopped speaking for a few moments, and all Gaby could think of was that there was nothing between him and Kate, and never had been. The secret whisper in her heart was singing its own wild song, beguiling her into believing things her mind couldn't quite accept. Frantically she tried to silence her heart by reminding herself that there'd been no continuity in her own relationship with Callum, no true foundation, no real trust. She didn't dare look at him, afraid he would read in her eyes the hopes and doubts alternately lifting her and dashing her down, and draw his own conclusions.

She knew he was watching her closely, as though expecting some some sort of response, and when she didn't give it his attitude altered. Gone was his softness, and he continued in a brisk, impersonal way, 'Kate tried again on Sunday, but I'd accepted by then that Justin and I could never be real brothers, so I finished it. I told her I'd known almost from the beginning what she and Justin were up to, and that it would never work. She must have told Justin at the nightclub, which must have prompted his offer for the gatehouse as one last way of getting back at me.'

'A pretty petty way,' Gaby said. 'I can't believe he was reduced to that.'

'Is that another way of saying you don't believe what I've been telling you?'

'No. It has to be the truth because there's no reason why you should have to justify yourself to me.' Gaby hestitated, then admitted, 'I'm not sure why you've bothered, to be honest.'

'I'm beginning to wonder myself,' Callum replied, with a harshness that bewildered her more than ever. 'Let's say that, since you found yourself caught up in the middle of it all, I felt you were owed an explanation.'

It was dawning uncomfortably on Gaby that she was developing an alarming tendency towards tears whenever Callum snapped at her. Annoyed with herself as much as him, she snapped back defensively, 'It's easy to heap all the blame on Justin and Kate. Are you so lily-white and squeaky-clean yourself?'

'No, I'm not,' he snarled, as though she'd touched on a raw nerve. 'Is Harry Preston?'

The question seemed so irrelevant that it knocked her off balance. When she recovered, she exclaimed, 'Harry's got nothing to do with it!'

'He's got everything to do with it. He's the fool who let you come here on your own. If he's any kind of man he should know a girl like you on the loose can't help but stir things up.'

The injustice brought Gaby to her feet, angry colour flooding her cheeks. 'If you're looking for a fool, look at me. I'm the one who's stupidity itself—for putting up with you! You're never the same for two minutes in a row. Well, like you, I learn my lessons, and I've had enough!'

She stormed towards the door, but Callum was too quick for her. He caught her as she reached for the door-handle. She was spun round and enveloped in his burly arms. All coherent thought fled, and it was an effort to hang on to her temper, especially when her face was pressed gently but inexorably into the rough wool of his sweater—which was where she'd wanted to be ever since she'd clapped eyes on him that morning.

'I'm sorry,' he murmured contritely. 'I can only excuse myself by saying Justin isn't the only one who's had a hell of a weekend. Don't be mad at me. We were well on the way to being friends, and that's the way I want to keep it.'

Was that, she thought indignantly, a kiss he dropped on her hair? He had a nerve! But there was something so soothing, so debilitating, about being cradled in his arms that all the fight went out of her. Not the resentment, though, and she grumbled, 'You'll do anything to get what you want, won't you?'

'Yes.'

Gaby felt choked with tears. She sniffed them away and came to a decision. 'Well, you can have the gatehouse. It won't do Justin any good, only fuel his resentment. Since Sam Gibson's already made enough money out of you, I'll sell it to you direct, as soon as I get an independent valuation. Will that make you happy?'

'No.'

Gaby prised herself out of his sweater and stared up at him. 'What do you mean, no? You're dead set on recovering all the original estate, and the gatehouse is the last missing piece.'

'Yes, but I think it will break you up to sell it.'

His blue eyes seemed to be seeing into her soul. Gaby was so overwhelmed that he instinctively understood how she felt that tears choked her again. Dismayed, she lowered her gaze to his sweater, seeing each individual fibre of wool and yet seeing nothing at all.

'You love the place, don't you, Gaby?'

She nodded, afraid to trust her voice.

'Then don't let Harry Preston push you into selling. If he loves you, he won't pressure you into parting with something you love—however impractical keeping it might be.'

Innate fairness made Gaby murmur, 'That's not really the way it is.'

'Isn't it?' Callum sounded unconvinced. 'Well, I'm not leaning on you. Just make sure nobody else does.'

She was so touched by his concern that she couldn't reply. Perhaps Callum realised it, because his tone lightened and he smiled. 'We're supposed to be riding this afternoon. The horses will be saddled up by now, if you're ready.'

Callum held out his hand, and without hesitation she took it. It seemed to clinch something, somehow, although not for the life of her could she have said exactly what.

CHAPTER TEN

THEY rode along the beach, Gaby on the grey gelding Callum kept as a companion horse for his big blue roan, which she'd first seen Justin riding. The tide was out and they galloped over the damp hard-packed sand as she'd once imagined galloping with Justin. She felt no pang of regret. The secret whisper in her heart wasn't in any doubt that being with Callum far surpassed her dead dreams of Justin.

She thought fleetingly that if the gossips were busy linking her and Justin they would be baffled now, because that day set the pattern for the rest of the week.

She and Callum would work in the morning, lunch together, then go riding, swimming or simply walking, depending how the mood took them. After that Callum would return to the manor and she to the gatehouse, and she would have to live as best she could through the empty hours until morning came. He never asked her to dine with him or suggested they spend an evening together.

Loving him, she was hurt immeasurably that he could shut her out of his mind when she was always emotionally tied to him. He seemed to have forgotten the living flame that leapt between them whenever they were in each other's arms, forcing her to believe his desire for her had died with the rivalry between him and Justin. She realised too late that she should have kept him guessing about her feelings for Justin.

As it was, he'd lost all sexual interest in her now

167

there were no obstacles between them. She didn't count Harry, because he was a distant problem that bothered her not at all. She could see what she hadn't been able to see before—how colourless and tame her relationship with him had been. Ending it was unlikely to cause Harry any more pain than it would cause her.

Gaby wanted to tell Callum about Harry, but he never mentioned him, and she didn't know how to. She was afraid that explaining she was heart-free might make Callum think she was throwing herself at him, and she couldn't have borne that. Harry seemed to have become the one taboo subject between them. They talked about everything else under the sun, and so frequently about Shorelands that she often wondered if it was the only bond they shared.

At other times she was certain they shared a great deal more than that, only to have her hopes dashed when Callum deliberately distanced himself. He seemed determined to treat her like some kind of favourite kid sister. She couldn't help but notice how he avoided touching her. She frequently felt like kicking him, or screaming with frustration. She yearned for his assaults, even his insults—anything rather than this sexless, soul-destroying friendship.

All in all, Gaby was being driven slowly up the wall, and yet she couldn't break free. The bittersweet torment of being with Callum was preferable to the private hell of being without him. But tension was mounting within her, and daily she dreaded his taking his usual weekly trip to London. Shorelands would mean nothing to her without him.

By Thursday lunchtime she'd convinced herself he wasn't leaving, and she was just beginning to relax when he said, 'I'm going to London tomorrow. I'll be back Saturday.'

Gaby's heart turned to stone and she replied involuntarily, 'I'll miss you.'

'Come with me.'

Her eyes flew to his, wide, speculative. To her, those three words meant the difference between living and mere existing, but she'd no idea what they meant to him. She'd known Callum almost a week now, but she was no closer to reading his mind than she'd ever been. In fact, she felt as though she was going backwards.

'German is one of the languages you speak, isn't it?' he went on.

'Yes.'

'I'm entertaining three German businessmen to dinner at my house in Belgravia tomorrow evening. They're looking for finance to branch out in England. I'm interested, but I want to find out more about them personally, and I find the best way to do that is at home. There are less distractions than dining out. Their wives or girlfriends will be with them. I need a hostess to entertain them after dinner when their men and I will be talking business. They probably all speak English, but being able to speak to people in their own language is a distinct advantage.'

Gaby didn't need convincing about that, but Callum was so impersonal about the invitation that she couldn't flatter herself he had any designs on her body. Rancour as much as anything prompted her to ask, 'I suppose that's the sort of job Kate does for you?'

'Did for me,' he corrected. 'Will you step in?'

Gaby thought he took altogether too much for granted, and she grumbled, 'You've left it late enough to ask. I might want to get my hair done or something.'

'Your hair always looks beautiful, and I thought you'd need time to learn that you can trust me. We'll leave at midday tomorrow.'

She cherished the compliment and hated being told she could trust him, which mixed her up so much that she snapped, 'I haven't agreed yet!'

'When women start talking about their hair it's a foregone conclusion.'

His smugness infuriated her. 'Do you know how hateful you can be, Callum Durand?'

'I'm trying to improve. Tell me when you're pleased with me and I'll know I'm doing something right.'

Gaby caught her breath. The way he was smiling suggested he was flirting with her, but she decided he must be teasing. She changed the subject, knowing that if she teased back he would retreat. She recognised the pattern by now. That didn't explain why he was so moody when they went riding after lunch, forcing her to return to the safe subject of Shorelands as they walked the horses to the stables after a gallop along the beach. 'Do you remember that map I found of Shorelands, Callum? Well, I've found another dated fifty years later, and one of the farms is on it. I think they should be framed and hung in the libary. If you agree, we could take them to London with us to be done.'

'I agree they should be framed, but not in London. I prefer to use local craftsmen whenever I can.'

Gaby grinned at him. 'Good thinking, squire. I'm beginning to see why you've become so popular around here.'

Callum neither grinned back nor answered. Either he read something into her remark that she didn't mean, or something else was eating him. Whatever it was, she wasn't the only one suffering from tension. She couldn't be, not if even Shorelands had ceased to be a safe subject between them.

* * *

The drive down to London in the sleek Jaguar was a mixed blessing for Gaby. She was glad to be close to Callum, and yet he'd never seemed more unattainable. He treated her as though she were a business associate, with pleasant but impersonal attentiveness. Something within her seemed to be withering and dying. She thought it was hope.

His house in Belgravia was tall, narrow, one of a gracious terrace built in the first half of the last century. She was surprised how large it was inside. It took her a while to figure out that it was because its depth was so much greater than its width.

The housekeeper, Mrs McEwen, was as welcoming as she was efficient. Gaby was a little embarrassed at first at having to check her arrangements for the dinner party, but she was able to relax when she could find no fault with the menu, the table setting, the wines or the flowers. Mrs McEwen seemed to like her, too, which helped. Gaby was very conscious that the older, sophisticated Kate Armstrong was a tough act to follow.

She bathed and dressed carefully for the dinner party in a dress of floating lemon chiffon over clinging lemon crêpe. The sleeves were full and the neckine dropped to show the line of her neck and shoulders. It was a dreamy rather than sensual style, and she pinned up her hair to make her look older. She knew the lemon set off the rich colouring of her hair and eyes, and that she had never looked better, but she still felt nervous when she went downstairs to join Callum.

She found him in the drawing-room drinking a pre-dinner sherry and her heart did one of the crazy somersaults she was somehow trying to learn to live with. Callum in a dinner suit looked so distinguished, but in a far sexier way than Harry had ever done. Her mind, as though it wanted to be absolutely sure of her

reactions, flipped from Harry to Justin. No, Callum
would never be quite as handsome as Justin, but he
would always be so much more manly—and she wanted
him so much!

Her feelings put a certain wistfulness in her smile as
she said, 'I've done my best. I hope I pass muster.'

Callum came towards her and his expression made
her catch her breath. She thought he was going to kiss
her, but she was mistaken. He pulled the pins from her
elaborately arranged chignon and her glossy hair tum-
bled to her shoulders. 'Callum, it took me ages to get
it up!' she protested.

'A waste of time. Your hair's too lovely to hide.' He
turned her to face an elegant giltwood wall-mirror.
'That's how I like to see you, how you should always
look.'

Gaby met Callum's eyes in the mirror. They were
warm, soft. Lover's eyes, she thought, her nerves
jumping and her pulses leaping. Afraid to believe what
she was sensing, she said inanely, 'I look too unsophis-
ticated with my hair down. Harry says so.'

'Sophisticated girls are ten a penny. You're an
original. If your Harry can't appreciate that, he's not
the man for you.'

Gaby wanted to say she knew he wasn't, but Callum
was turning away. He went over to the decanters on a
sideboard and poured her a sherry. The barrier was
down between them again and she felt forlorn. She
tried to hide it by saying lightly, 'You're very kind,
Callum, but I think Harry's right. I'm not beautiful. I
I don't have style, I don't have anything.'

'Kind?' Callum slammed down the decanter and
swung to face her. 'I'm not being kind, I'm being
honest. You have your own style, and Harry Preston
must be mad to try to destroy it. As for beauty, there's

the kind the camera loves and there's the other kind—glowing, vital, unique. The one's an image, the other's priceless. You must love Preston very much to let him destroy the person you really are.'

Was this a friend who had her best interests at heart speaking, or was it the furious outpouring of a frustrated lover? Gaby had no idea, she only knew she couldn't play safe any longer. 'I don't love Harry,' she said.

'Then who the hell kept you out of Justin's bed? I don't know any other girls who've managed it.'

'You.'

There was silence. It was complete enough for Gaby to hear her own heart pounding in her ears, and it went on long enough for shame to flood her. Her pride tasted like ashes in her mouth.

'Me?' Callum sounded dazed, as well he might.

Gaby hung her head. She was glad her hair was loose now, because it fell forward to hide her flaming cheeks. 'Forget I said that,' she mumbled. 'I didn't mean to.'

She heard Callum coming towards her and felt his hands on her hair, but very warily, as though he wasn't sure whether he had the right. That seemed very strange to her. When had he bothered whether or not he had the right? 'Look at me, Gaby,' he said.

'No.'

He forced her face up to his. 'Are you saying it's me you love? Tell me, Gaby!'

She summoned up a cheeky smile from somewhere. It was the hardest thing she'd ever done, since she felt much more like dying. 'Certainly not,' she managed spiritedly. 'I make it a practice never to make a fool of myself twice in one evening.'

His head came down and he kissed her very gently on the lips. The sweetest, most weakening sensation suffused her entire body. 'Oh, Callum, play fair,' she murmured brokenly.

He looked searchingly at her. 'Are you sure you're playing fair?' he asked. She didn't know what he meant, but it didn't seem to matter because he swept her into his arms, saying, 'Oh, to hell with it! I love you. I'll take you any way I can get you.'

He kissed her in a way that drove all outside thought from her mind. She forgot his guests were due to arrive, and didn't care that her frail chiffon dress was being crushed. The world had shrunk to the two of them, and it was enough. It was Callum who came to his senses first. Reluctantly he put her away from him and led her over to the telephone. He picked up the receiver and held it out to her. 'Phone Preston and tell him how things are,' he ordered. 'I can't live with the feeling that I'm sharing you.'

'You're not sharing me.' Gaby took the receiver from him and replaced it in its cradle. 'It wasn't a physical relationship, or even an emotional one. Harry and I were compatible as business associates, and we were building on it from there.' She paused, too shy to explain about the secret whisper in her heart that had always stopped her from settling for less than the feeling she was capable of.

Conscious that Callum was waiting for an explanation, she hurried on, 'We never could have been compatible as lovers. I think I always knew it, and that's why I returned to Shorelands. The gatehouse was just an excuse, although I didn't properly realise it until I arrived. Then I had to face the fact that there was so much of me Harry didn't know about, and wouldn't approve of if he did. What really happened was that I stopped wanting to please him, and there was nothing left. As an employer, though, he was very

ood to me, always careful not to take liberties. He
eserves more than a phone call. I'll explain face to
ace what's happened when he returns to England.'

'So that's how it was.' Curiously, Callum didn't look
elieved. 'Your heart's always been at Shorelands,
asn't it?'

He was tracing her lips thoughtfully and, tantalised,
he kissed his fingers before she admitted, 'One way or
nother. Is that bad?'

Callum seemed to hesitate fractionally. Then he
olded her into his arms and buried his face in her hair.
Nothing can be as bad as this past week,' he mur-
aured, as though he'd come to a decision about
omething. 'I've been going out of my mind trying to
eep my hands off you. I've been rationing myself with
our company, you know. I didn't dare see you in the
venings in case I lost control.'

'Oh, Callum, I never guessed!' Gaby could have
ept when she thought of those endless evenings and
he empty nights. 'I thought you were making sure the
ardener's granddaughter knew her place.'

He shook her roughly, then made up for it by kissing
er. 'Don't ever think like that,' he ordered. 'I was
rying to make a place for myself. I knew Justin had
ut his own throat, but I thought I'd done the same.
've been trying to give you time to get to know me
roperly. I fixed up this dinner tonight especially to get
s away from Shorelands so we could have a fresh
tart.'

Whatever doubts Gaby had had were laid to rest.
Callum was speaking like a lover, and a desperate one.
Her eyes misted, but, rather than cry all over his
mmaculate dinner shirt, she laughed and said none-
oo-steadily, 'You went to a lot of trouble for nothing.

If you've been looking for a soft spot, you of all people should know you can't beat Shorelands.'

Callum raised his head and looked at her with an expression she couldn't read. She felt a flicker of panic, knowing she'd said the wrong thing, but not knowing why. All at once it came to her how little she really knew about this man she loved, and what she did know wasn't exactly reassuring. He'd proved how unfeeling he could be by taking Shorelands from Justin.

There were any amount of country estates he could have bought, without shattering all Justin's hopes. Perhaps Justin wouldn't be drinking and womanising so much if Callum hadn't prevented him from regaining his birthright. Gaby was human enough to acknowledge the motivation of an older, ignored and bastard brother, and yet woman enough to wish he could have risen above spite and revenge.

It was a measure of her love that she could know all this about Callum and still love him, whereas her dreams of Justin had crumbled to nothing when he'd proved to be less than her ideal. It was the man she loved, not a hero on a pedestal, and it made her feel very vulnerable.

'Callum,' she said uncertainly, 'what is it? Sometimes I feel you're disappointed in me, and I don't know——'

She got no further. Callum's lips crushed hers ruthlessly, as if seeking by force the answer to another question entirely. Gaby's senses reeled and she lost track of what she'd been saying. She only partially remembered when he said thickly, 'I love you. How could I possibly be disappointed? I just need to know you love me.'

'I love you,' she said hastily, placating a demon

within Callum which she scarcely understood. 'I truly do.'

His face lightened and he smiled, making her senses reel in an entirely different way. No, he would never be as classically handsome as Justin, but he would always be infinitely more dear. 'That's all that matters,' he said. 'To hell with everything else.'

What 'else' was there? Gaby wondered, but she was too overwhelmed at finding herself loved to think it through. Nothing mattered but the two of them—or didn't until the doorbell pealed. 'Oh, my gosh!' she exclaimed, pulling herself out of his arms. 'Your guests, and I must look a mess.'

'*Our* guests, and you look beautiful.'

Gaby was hurrying to check her appearance in the giltwood wall-mirror. 'I'm not beautiful,' she said wistfully, wanting so much to be beautiful for Callum. 'I'm just me.'

'I can't think of anything more beautiful than that.'

He meant it, he really did, and Gaby knew then what it was to *feel* beautiful. Impulsively she ran back to him and flung herself into his arms, hugging him and exclaiming, 'I love you for saying that, and I'll take you round to the optician's first thing in the morning.'

Callum laughed, but was quickly serious again. 'I take it we're engaged, Gaby?'

'Oh.' She hadn't thought that far ahead, hadn't dared to. She said shyly, 'If you're sure.'

'You're the one who has to be sure.'

She smiled tremulously. 'Then we're engaged,' she said, and surrendered once more to his kisses.

It was a very dishevelled Gaby who stood beside Callum to greet their guests, but it didn't matter because she was radiant. He introduced her as his fiancée, and that more than anything else convinced her all this was really happening. Her happiness spilled over everywhere, embracing the three businessmen and their wives, so that the evening was a runaway success.

She basked in Callum's approval, and to know she was also useful to him added a fillip to her happiness. At last the two sides of her—the businesswoman and the dreamy girl who'd never quite grown up—had come together, and it was Callum who had made it happen.

He was what her heart had been whispering about all these years. Justin, Harry and the other men she'd known had just been necessary experiences along a road that had always been leading to Callum. She loved him so honestly, so completely; she didn't think she'd ever learn to cope with the joy of finding that she, too, was loved. No wonder her heart was beating so deliriously. She was in a fever.

She knew the cure, and as soon as they'd closed the front door on their guests she turned straight into Callum's arms, pressing her soft body against his, leaning her head against his shoulder and closing her eyes so she could experience the sweet joy of belonging.

Callum's response was immediate and fierce. His arms tightened around her and he said thickly, 'I want you, Gaby. You know that, don't you?'

'Yes.' She had no thought for guile or teasing. 'I want you, too.'

He picked her up. She wound her arms around his shoulders and pressed loving kisses against his neck and ear as he carried her up the stairs. 'I'll drop you if you keep that up,' he murmured threateningly, but Gaby laughed, feeling safer in his arms than she'd ever felt in her life.

It was when he put her down in his bedroom that she began to feel unsafe, but deliciously so. The soft crêpe and floating chiffon of her dress flattened to nothing under his exploring hands, but it was a barrier he was impatient of. As he searched for the cunningly concealed zip she took off his dinner-jacket, tie and shirt. Her hands were roaming over his bare shoulders when her dress fell like a spreading yellow cloud to her feet.

He pressed her against him and the fever consuming her burst into flame as her bare breasts touched his chest. She gasped and clung to him. She had felt desire before, but never anything like this, incapable of check or control. Callum turned her face up to his and began to kiss her searchingly. One of his hands was tangled in her hair, the other was moving possessively over her body, lighting further fires wherever he touched.

'Gaby, you said Harry wasn't your lover. Were there any others?' he asked huskily.

She shook her head, incapable of speech because his hand had found her breast and was doing unspeakably delicious things to her hardened nipple. It was a torment she could scarcely endure and yet never wanted to stop. She hardly heard him continue, 'Then I'm a lucky man. Oh, Gaby, my little darling, I do love you so.'

She managed to whisper, 'I love you. So much. . .'

She was lifted off her feet and placed in the middle of his big bed. Then he was kissing her breasts, his tongue flickering over her nipples until she writhed in a further torment of ecstasy. 'Callum!' she moaned, but he knew it was no real protest and he didn't stop.

Gaby felt him undoing her suspenders and removing her stockings. Her panties followed them, and he removed the last of his own clothes. She was longing to feel his hard body crush hers, but his lips were

following his hands down her body and fresh waves o
pleasure flamed through her.

She was ready to beg for a release from the almos
agonised ecstasy he had aroused in her when he parte
her legs and moved over her. She clutched at hi
shoulders and cried out as he thrust again and agai
into her, but the pain was swiftly followed by th
unutterable pleasure of knowing she truly belonged t
him now.

Instinctively she moved with him, and he gasped, s
that she knew she was giving him pleasure, too. As h
climaxed she knew the incredible joy of being s
wanted, so needed. It was all too much. Tears trickle
down her face as he collapsed against her, and sh
cradled his head lovingly against her breasts.

'Gaby,' he said brokenly. 'Gaby. . .'

'Shush,' she said softly, knowing she was the one i
control now, the one who had the words. 'You don'
have to say a thing. You just have to go to sleep.'

Callum did fall asleep, too, right where he was. Gab
stayed awake for a while, smoothing his damp hai
back from his forehead and smiling into the darkness
Callum was hers, she was his—and her heart wa
singing of a happiness beyond the imaginings of he
wildest, most wilful dreams.

Callum made love to her again the next morning
tenderly—a totally different mood and experience, bu
just as magical. As they lay in each other's arm
afterwards, he kissed her forehead and asked, 'Wha
do you want to do today—stay in London or go bac
to Shorelands?'

'Shorelands,' Gaby said without hesitation. It ha
always been her special place. How much more specia
it would be now. . .

'I knew you'd say that.' Callum eased her out of his arms and got out of bed.

Again Gaby had the feeling she'd said the wrong thing, and she couldn't imagine why. Callum loved Shorelands as much as she did. That was why he'd cut Justin out in the first place—or said he had. Troubled, he sat up and caught his arm. 'If you don't want to go to Shorelands——' she began, and got no further.

Callum bent and kissed the rest of her words away. 'You're happiest at Shorelands so that's where we're going—only we won't be going anywhere if you look at me with your eyes wide open like that, my little owl.'

She laughed and the tiny cloud that had sailed across her happiness vanished. She must have imagined that sudden reserve in Callum, probably because she hadn't quite learned to accept he loved her as unconditionally as she loved him.

Everything they did that day seemed to be leisurely—bathing, dressing, breakfasting, driving home. They were in their own enchanted world and nobody was standing by with a stop-watch. They had so much to discover about each other, so much to talk about, so much to plan.

As they finally topped the rise and looked down at the wide and shallow valley that was Shorelands, Callum said, 'I've got a motor cruiser at Beccles. How do you feel about spending the rest of the weekend on the Broads?'

He sounded casual, but Gaby knew for certain then that he didn't want to be with her at Shorelands. It hurt immeasurably, too much to ask why, and she replied, 'It sounds fun.'

'Sure?'

It hurt to smile, too, but she made a good job of i
'Certain.'

They stopped at the gatehouse for Gaby to chang
and repack her weekend bag, then drove on to th
manor. Callum went upstairs to get ready. Mrs Hoskin
wasn't about, so Gaby went to the records room. Sh
wanted a little privacy to explore this new hurt with
her, to consider whether it was real or imaginary. Sh
found the two maps that were to be framed and hur
in the library.

Restless, she took them down and put them c
Callum's desk. Looking for a safer place, she opened
desk drawer to see if there was room. She wasn't real
thinking what she was doing; she just needed to kee
her hands busy while her mind probed into places
didn't really want to go.

She found herself staring at a thick sheaf of pape
labelled 'Shorelands Development Plan: Phases 1–5
For a few blank seconds her brain refused to registe
what her eyes were reading, then ice seemed to sprea
all over her. With fingers that shook slightly, she lifte
out the papers and began to look through them.

Her first glance showed her this was a provision
outline for the development of Shorelands into
massive housing complex. Phase One covered conver
ing the manor into flats, and its barns and outbuildin
into 'character' residences; the paddock would be th
site of 'prestige' houses and the agricultural land wou
be transferred to Lower Mead Farm. Secondary deve
opments would be bungalows on either side of th
main drive, within the belt of trees to pacify conserv.
tionists, and on either side of the gatehouse driv
Gaby, disbelieving, studied the plan and saw that
bungalow was even sited in her garden.

Phase Two covered linking the separate bungalo

levelopments with country-cottage-style houses. Terraced houses were to be built on the boundaries of the wo farms where they ran alongside the road, and the paddock development was to be extended. If there was a public outcry against the loss of agricultural land, the marshes were to be filled in to provide more.

Horrified, Gaby flicked through the next two phases and looked at the last. The manor stood in a couple of acres of green. All the rest, including the farms, was a mass of houses from the main road to the sea. There were small artificial 'village greens' here and there, and patches of woodland, amounting to little more than a sop to those who would protest.

The whole thing was cunningly phased over a period of years to get planning permission bit by bit. Gaby knew the syndrome. Establish one small development and the rest followed with sickening regularity. What she was looking at here was the cold-blooded destruction of a beautiful estate that had survived virtually intact from medieval times, and the obliteration of its teeming wildlife.

And Callum, her darling Callum, was the one who was going to do it. Why? For some dreadful revenge on the father who'd disowned him, or purely for profit? But Callum didn't need money, not unless he was motivated by an insatiable greed.

Gaby felt as though her world was reeling. She collapsed weakly into Callum's chair and the papers fell from her nerveless fingers on to the desk. She looked at the papers with revulsion and pushed them alway as though they were tainted.

Callum had lied when he'd said he'd bought Shorelands because he loved it. He had lied when he'd promised the woods and marshes would always be protected, and he had lied about caring so much about

the land that he was switching to organic farmin
Everything had been a lie—except for loving her. Sh
knew it would be rational to doubt that, too, and y
she also knew no two people could be the way the
were together unless the love was sincere on both side

With a groan, Gaby rested her elbows on the de
and buried her face in her hands. She was hopeless
in love with a man who was her natural enemy,
spoiler of everything her deepest instincts compelle
her to protect. 'Oh, Callum,' she whispered, 'ho
could you?'

His hand came down on her hair in that lovin
tender way she'd come to know so well. She hadn
heard him come into the room, and she jumped an
recoiled. Callum withdrew his hand and stood lookin
down at her, his expression impossible to read.

'I was looking for a safe place to put the maps.
found these,' Gaby said dully. She picked up the she
of papers and threw it contemptuously at him. F
didn't attempt to catch it, and it fluttered to his fee
Gaby stood up, needing to get away from him whil
she got herself under control. Imagine her needing
get away from Callum! Her heart seemed to be dyin
within her, leaving her shell to survive as best it coul
if it had a will to. Now she understood why Callum w
uneasy about her being at Shorelands. Having wo
her, he had to wean her away from the estate befo
he could put his devious and destructive plans in
effect.

She went to the french windows and stared ou
visualising the rolling countryside beyond the pat
garden, green and open to the wide blue sky. As it ha
been for centuries, and would be for very little longer

'Gaby. . .' Callum said, moving towards her.

'I'm not very safe at the moment,' she replied
ercely. 'Stay away from me.'

'No, I can't do that. After last night, I can't imagine
ny situation in which you'd want to stay away from
1e. Am I wrong about that?'

Gaby rounded on him savagely. 'You know I love
horelands!'

'More than me?'

He was so close to her. She was weakening and she
ated herself for it. She shook her head, as much in
espair as anger. 'No,' she replied at last. 'God help
1e, I love you more than I could ever love anything or
nybody else, but——'

'Gaby. . .' Callum took her face gently in his hands
nd kissed her.

She was powerless to resist his lips, but when he
aised them she continued, '——but I'll fight you for
very last inch of Shorelands I can save, and I'll fight
irty. When you put up Phase One for planning
ermission, I'll tell about all the other phases. I'll rally
very conservationist, every animal lover, every bird
over, every tree lover, every local person who doesn't
ant their environment spoiled, and anybody any-
here who'll petition against you. I swear, Callum, I'll
o my damnedest to stop you before you start. Are
ou sure you still want to marry me?'

'I've told you once that I'm sure, and I'm not a man
ho changes his mind.' Callum folded her into his
rms. He felt her stiffness, her resistance. He bent and
issed her ear. She melted a little, but not a lot. 'What
wasn't sure about was you and Shorelands,' he went
n. 'I know how fiercely you love the place, and I
1ought you might have persuaded yourself you loved
1e because of it. It was rotten being jealous of
2mething I own, and my pride wouldn't let me take

second place to anything. Then——' Callum sighe
turned her face up to his and kissed her again. 'Ther
he continued, 'my love for you got too much to contro
I had to swallow my pride and my doubts and take yo
any way I could get you. . .the way I know now you'
prepared to take me. And I love you for it, Gaby,
very much.'

Gaby, awed that he could love her so much, wante
to cry, but that didn't stop her wanting to cry ov
Shorelands as well. 'I can't change the person I ar
Callum. I'll have to fight you over the development.
won't be able to help myself.'

'I wouldn't let you change, and there isn't going
be a fight. We're on the same side.' He picked her v
and carried her over to a sofa, and sat with her cradle
in his arms.

She stared up at him, happiness glowing in her brov
eyes. 'You mean you'll drop the scheme?'

'It wasn't mine in the first place. It was Justin's.
didn't buy Shorelands to ruin it, but to save it, ar
that's why he can't forgive me. I've stopped hi
making millions.'

'Justin's?' Gaby couldn't believe her ears. 'But
thought the health farm was his way of making
financially independent so he could keep it!'

'That was just a blind. The Hazletts had no idea
the potential worth of Shorelands, and they we
selling by private treaty to Justin because he was
Durand. The consortium had to keep absolutely secr
about their plans, because if any big developer had g
wind of it they wouldn't have been able to compete.'

'Then Kate brought you here,' Gaby guessed.

'Yes. I did fall in love with Shorelands, but Just
had the greater claim, having been born and reare
here. I looked around for another property, and whe

went to Gibson's I met Amanda. Sam was out. I took
Amanda to lunch while I outlined what I was looking
or. Then she told me just what Justin, Gibson and a
ew others were up to.'

'Amanda did? Sam thinks it was the char, Mrs Foley,
who was the spy in camp!' Gaby exclaimed.

'I know, but I was able to look after Mrs Foley when
am fired her, so there was no harm done there. It was
ustin's womanising that was his undoing. He had an
ffair with Amanda, then dropped her, as he's dropped
ll the others. She got back at him the only way she
ould—through Shorelands. She slipped me a copy of
he development plans, and that's when I stepped in
nd bought it.'

Gaby said slowly, 'It's unbelievable, what Justin was
oing to do to Shorelands. He was *raised* here, just as
is ancestors have been for nearly three hundred years.
t's—it's almost sacrilege, and I thought he loved the
lace.'

'Not as much as he loves the high life—and that was
ur father's downfall as well. Properly managed,
horelands can support itself comfortably, but it can't
tretch to too many fast cars, yachts and Bermudan
olidays.'

'Why have you covered up for Justin? Most local
eople hate change, and they'd have accepted you far
lore readily if they'd known what he was planning to
o,' Gaby said.

Callum shrugged. 'He's my brother. I thought in
me we might come to some kind of understanding. I
as wrong.'

Gaby's hand strayed to his face. 'Well, I'm glad I at
east know the truth now, although it was awful of me
o think such dreadful things about you. I should have
nown better. I'm so sorry.'

He took her hand and kissed the palm. 'I'm not. gave me the chance to find out what I really wanted know.'

Callum began to kiss each of her fingers individuall sending delightful shivers all over her body. He w teasing her, and he knew it, but Gaby didn't care. F was her darling man again, and he always would b 'How do I know you're not marrying me just to get t gatehouse?' she asked provocatively.

'You don't, but that's the least of your worries. I' got far more Machiavellian schemes in mind for you he threatened.

'Wicked squire,' she murmured, drawing his hand her lips and beginning to nibble his thumb. 'Wh chance does the poor little gardener's granddaught have?'

'None at all,' Callum said, abandoning her finge and beginning to kiss her in earnest.

Take 4 bestselling love stories FREE

Plus get a FREE surprise gift!

Special Limited-time Offer

Mail to
Harlequin Reader Service®
3010 Walden Avenue
P.O. Box 1867
Buffalo, N.Y. 14269-1867

YES! Please send me 4 free Harlequin Presents® novels and my free surprise gift. Then send me 6 brand-new novels every month, which I will receive months before they appear in bookstores. Bill me at the low price of $2.47 each—a savings of 28¢ apiece off cover prices. There are no shipping, handling or other hidden costs. I understand that accepting the books and gift places me under no obligation ever to buy any books. I can always return a shipment and cancel at any time. Even if I never buy another book from Harlequin, the 4 free books and the surprise gift are mine to keep forever.

106 BPA AC9K

Name	(PLEASE PRINT)	
Address		Apt. No.
City	State	Zip

This offer is limited to one order per household and not valid to present Harlequin Presents® subscribers. Terms and prices are subject to change.
Sales tax applicable in N.Y.

PRES-BPA2DR   © 1990 Harlequin Enterprises Limited

HARLEQUIN®
OFFICIAL SWEEPSTAKES RULES

NO PURCHASE NECESSARY

To enter, complete an Official Entry Form or 3"× 5" index card by hand-printing, in plain block letters, your complete name, address, phone number and age, and mailing it to: Harlequin Fashion A Whole New You Sweepstakes, P.O. Box 9056, Buffalo, NY 14269-9056.

No responsibility is assumed for lost, late or misdirected mail. Entries must be sent separately with first class postage affixed, and be received no later than December 31, 1991 for eligibility.

Winners will be selected by D.L. Blair, Inc., an independent judging organization whose decisions are final, in random drawings to be held on January 30, 1992 in Blair, NE at 10:00 a.m. from among all eligible entries received.

The prizes to be awarded and their approximate retail values are as follows: Grand Prize — A brand-new Mercury Sable LS plus a trip for two (2) to Paris, including round-trip air transportation, six (6) nights hotel accommodation, a $1,400 meal/spending money stipend and $2,000 cash toward a new fashion wardrobe (approximate value: $28,000) or $15,000 cash; two (2) Second Prizes — A trip to Paris, including round-trip air transportation, six (6) nights hotel accommodation, a $1,400 meal/spending money stipend and $2,000 cash toward a new fashion wardrobe (approximate value: $11,000) or $5,000 cash; three (3) Third Prizes — $2,000 cash toward a new fashion wardrobe. All prizes are valued in U.S. currency. Travel award air transportation is from the commercial airport nearest winner's home. Travel is subject to space and accommodation availability, and must be completed by June 30, 1993. Sweepstakes offer is open to residents of the U.S. and Canada who are 21 years of age or older as of December 31, 1991, except residents of Puerto Rico, employees and immediate family members of Torstar Corp., its affiliates, subsidiaries, and all agencies, entities and persons connected with the use, marketing, or conduct of this sweepstakes. All federal, state, provincial, municipal and local laws apply. Offer void wherever prohibited by law. Taxes and/or duties, applicable registration and licensing fees, are the sole responsibility of the winners. Any litigation within the province of Quebec respecting the conduct and awarding of a prize may be submitted to the Régie des loteries et courses du Québec. All prizes will be awarded; winners will be notified by mail. No substitution of prizes is permitted.

Potential winners must sign and return any required Affidavit of Eligibility/Release of Liability within 30 days of notification. In the event of noncompliance within this time period, the prize may be awarded to an alternate winner. Any prize or prize notification returned as undeliverable may result in the awarding of that prize to an alternate winner. By acceptance of their prize, winners consent to use of their names, photographs or their likenesses for purposes of advertising, trade and promotion on behalf of Torstar Corp. without further compensation. Canadian winners must correctly answer a time-limited arithmetical question in order to be awarded a prize.

For a list of winners (available after 3/31/92), send a separate stamped, self-addressed envelope to: Harlequin Fashion A Whole New You Sweepstakes, P.O. Box 4694, Blair, NE 68009.

PREMIUM OFFER TERMS

To receive your gift, complete the Offer Certificate according to directions. Be certain to enclose the required number of "Fashion A Whole New You" proofs of product purchase (which are found on the last page of every specially marked "Fashion A Whole New You" Harlequin or Silhouette romance novel). Requests must be received no later than December 31, 1991. Limit: four (4) gifts per name, family, group, organization or address. Items depicted are for illustrative purposes only and may not be exactly as shown. Please allow 6 to 8 weeks for receipt of order. Offer good while quantities of gifts last. In the event an ordered gift is no longer available, you will receive a free, previously unpublished Harlequin or Silhouette book for every proof of purchase you have submitted with your request, plus a refund of the postage and handling charge you have included. Offer good in the U.S. and Canada only.

HQFW · SWPR

HARLEQUIN® OFFICIAL SWEEPSTAKES ENTRY FORM

4-FWHR

Complete and return this Entry Form immediately – the m
entries you submit, the better your chances of winning!

- Entries must be received by **December 31, 1991.**
- A Random draw will take place on **January 30, 1992**
- No purchase necessary.

Yes, I want to win a FASHION A WHOLE NEW YOU Classic and Romantic prize from Harleq

Name _____ Telephone _____ Age ____

Address _____

City _____ State _____ Zip _____

Return Entries to: **Harlequin FASHION A WHOLE NEW YOU,**
P.O. Box 9056, Buffalo, NY 14269-9056   © 1991 Harlequin Enterprises Lin

PREMIUM OFFER

To receive your free gift, send us the required number of proofs-of-purchase from any speci
marked FASHION A WHOLE NEW YOU Harlequin or Silhouette Book with the Offer Certific
properly completed, plus a check or money order (do not send cash) to cover postage and hand
payable to Harlequin FASHION A WHOLE NEW YOU Offer. We will send you the specified g

OFFER CERTIFICATE

Item	A. ROMANTIC COLLECTOR'S DOLL (Suggested Retail Price $60.00)	B. CLASSIC PICTU FRAME (Suggested Retail Price $29
# of proofs-of-purchase	18	12
Postage and Handling	$3.50	$2.95
Check one	☐	☐

Name _____

Address _____

City _____ State _____ Zip _____

Mail this certificate, designated number of proofs-of-purchase and check or money order
postage and handling to: **Harlequin FASHION A WHOLE NEW YOU Gift Offer**, P.O. Box 90
Buffalo, NY 14269-9057. Requests must be received by December 31, 1991.

ONE PROOF-OF-PURCHASE

4-FWHRP-2

To collect your fabulous free gift you must include
the necessary number of proofs-of-purchase with
a properly completed Offer Certificate.

© 1991 Harlequin Enterprises Limite

See previous page for details.